END REALM

TYLER J. WELCH

Asphodel Press LLC
Beaver Dam, Wisconsin | tylerjwelch.com

End Realm
Copyright © 2024 by Tyler J. Welch

Published by Asphodel Press LLC
Beaver Dam, Wisconsin
www.tylerjwelch.com

Library of Congress Control Number: 2024908132

ISBN 979-8-9905586-0-1 (paperback)
ISBN 979-8-9905586-1-8 (hardcover)
ISBN 979-8-9905586-2-5 (ebook)

Cover art, design, and interior formatting by Nicole Welch
Asphodel Press logo by Nicole Welch

First Edition: 2024
Printed and bound by IngramSpark

"Death is end and beginning. Inciting fear in most, stories in some, life in all."

END REALM

CHAPTER ONE

Lost

I plummet through an eternal darkness, my hearing muffled like a suffocating dove. *Am I falling through the dark depths of an oceanic trench?* The uncomfortable pressure pains the drums of my ears. Fear strikes the core of my chest like a tsunami rapes a shoreline. Chills rush out in a race to my fingertips, just to give chase back to my core—a sick game fear is. My heart suddenly falls through my back, giving my spine a jolt. The abyssal ink gets pushed through by my hands and arms as I startle—that instinctual grasp-out to catch myself, catch myself from being swallowed, or perhaps to hastily turn around and catch my fallen heart as it plummets faster than I.

The pressure folds in, crushing me into a ball, and a scream of pain escapes my throat, a scream that I can hear. Solid ground against my palms now—cold. My chest heaves with what feels like the first breaths I've ever taken. My fall has stopped, but where?

"What the . . ." *No longer an eternal darkness.* ". . . fuck? Where am—"

A concussive slam from behind pushes the atmosphere past and through my hair. The fading tremors in the ground reverberate up into my knees, and it almost hurts. I am struck with surprise and unfamiliarity by the darkened landscape before me—jutting sections of shale all reaching for different heights, smooth twisting paths branching out in varying directions, mangrove-like trees in the distance blocking my view of the horizon. I become aware that I have no recollection of my surroundings nor how I got here, which allows a draft of unease to froth up and linger within my chest (another game fear likes to play).

I turn. Before me is a massive door resembling a slab of obsidian carved and etched in intricate Gothic designs that undoubtedly birthed the concussive slam. There are no handles but a large golden keylock, impossible to miss on the right-hand side. The door stands several stories tall and is laid out on a wall so vast that I can see no end regardless of the direction looked. In the awe I catch myself in, I drop whatever was apparently in my hand. Two golden coins fall and ring on the dark callous rock ground on which I stand. Picking them back up and inspecting them leads to my first discovery of this . . . place that I seem to recognize and somewhat understand.

I roll the coins over in my palm. The brassy golden material of each clacks against the other, each side inlaid with a carved pentagram, their orientation alternating.

These symbols, I know them . . .

I can't recall the source of this knowledge I possess, but I know what this is. A symbol of the natural order of things, a symbol of good faith, the changing seasons, a protection against evil, the reversed pentagram generally symbolizing the opposite—the unlawful order of the universe, chaos, and even evil of the world. It comes to me that I believe the two together really show perfection—how the universe and the people in it are both good and evil and can learn from both sides to better themselves. It feels awkward coming to this realization, however, as I have no memory of where or how the knowledge was acquired. My head shakes as I try to jostle loose memories of how I know this, but nothing comes. I feel lost. I inhale deeply.

"Just breathe, man. Breathe. You can figure this out."

Not knowing what the coins are or how they came into my possession, I feel it best to keep them. My only belongings. Yes, they must stay with me.

"Okay, now where the hell am I?"

I look around. The vast door and seemingly never-ending wall are clearly impenetrable. Opposite the vast wall, a view of darkness spreads out far and wide, and looking to the sky feels like being transported into a room of complete darkness with zero visibility. There are no stars, no clouds, nor any gradients to be found, as if there is no sky nor a ceiling at all. Just an over-bearing endless abyss. The core of my chest flickers with those waves again. *Goddammit. Fuck you, fear.*

Whatever calm I muster becomes fleeting. I am a grain of sand at the base of a door, an ant lost in a canyon. My breath snags. There's not enough air under this blanket of entrapment, this blanket that's impossible to shake or tear off my shoulders. I am physically in a world I have no recollection of, and at the same time, I am mentally displaced as well. I think hard—to no avail. I have zero memory of where I was prior to this or even who else I knew or had connections with. *Think. Think!*

Okay, I know of my species. I know I am human—a man in my third decade of life. I know there was a world I lived in, where there was a large population of human communities. I have knowledge of how that world and those communities worked and intertwined together. I have an understanding of how those humans lived their lives and everything the world consisted of, from hate and love to geology and space exploration, to personal relationships and national politics. I know of all these aspects, yet any memory of who I was in that world? Gone. Lost to the oceanic abyss, just as I am. *Why can't I figure this out?*

Hollowness expands within my chest, causing my insides to feel cold and weightless. More anxiety.

I kneel down. I need to compose myself and figure this the fuck out! To get a better handle on my current physiologically

3

escalated and aroused state. If I don't, I am bound to make poor decisions and will most likely get myself in a worse situation, possibly even get hurt, or end up *dead*.

The distant sound of a bell ruptures the quiet still air. My eyes dart, and my head involuntarily tucks. Again, it rings, more distinct this time, sounding like a large brass instrument repeating itself several times in eerie cadence. The chime abrasively cuts through the constant calm, almost soothing breeze that seems to never waver. The sound of the bell—it's definitely getting more pronounced and the source closer. I let myself sit in the stillness, waiting and listening to the approach, though the anxiety and insects within my chest continue their disturbing dance.

There! The double chime is now a faint yellowish light. I can see it creeping through the dense tree branches just off in the distance. I get myself as low as possible, staying motionless as the source of light and sound gets closer, and then stop moving just inside a patch of twisted shrubs—the mangroves. The light ceases its advance but bobs and weaves side to side ever so slightly. The double chime of the bell keeps its cadence.

What are my options here? I think to myself.

Proceeding toward the light source, which I know nothing about, is to chase the unknown, and therefore, I find myself contemplating if it's worth the risk. Moreover, with nothing but a wall behind me and dark thicket ahead, I either follow the impenetrable wall away from the slaloming light (altogether avoidance being the goal) or the burning curiosity flowing through my very human veins is allowed to succeed in its enticement. A line about cats comes to mind.

How the hell does that go again? Ah, right, curiosity killed the cat. An almost inaudible chuckle rattles my throat. *Eh, they have nine lives anyway, right? Let's see what the cat finds . . . but slowly. No reason the damn cat needs to be stupid, right?* Plus, logically, anything meaning harm would generally not travel whilst making such a profound and cutting sound, nor would it be in its best interest to shed light in such an unlit environment. *Decision's been made.*

The smooth paths of stone ground that weave and flow like serpents around the jutting shards of sharp shale make most of the traversal easy, though ahead, I see clearer now just how treacherous the mangrove-like tree line is. Closer to a mangrove or a rhododendron—I am not sure; they are leafless and horrifically dense. It was far easier to keep an eye on the source of light from afar. Now I've lost sight. The maze I am faced with impedes my view. I make no attempt to traverse this clustered hell of mangrove silently. I want whatever's ahead to know of my presence. That is if there even is a form of life ahead. Either way, smartest to not startle or threaten anything unless threatened myself.

"Argh! Ouch," I say around a clenched jaw. Teeth hit my bottom lip. "The trees have thorns. Of course. Why wouldn't they?" I shake my head.

My palm sears slightly as the next branch meets my hand, this time slippery with blood. Again, the radiance comes into view and, with it, the end of the low twisted trees. There's a clearing ahead between me and the light source. I hop off and let go of the gripped branch. Smooth stone ground again. I exhale. Shoulders loosen, but then the insects in the chest return. I hadn't realized how barren this clearing is. Fifteen yards off at the far edge, clearly seen, is the source of amber light hanging from a small front mast on a wooden boat.

Next to the glass-encompassed light hangs a golden bell that resembles those found in a church, though this one's fitted for the small craft. I pace closer, squinting through the dim light and darkness beyond. My footfalls are near silent on the blackened clearing. Ahead is a slow serene moving river on which the wooden craft gently follows the motion of the water's ebb and flow. Sight of what—or rather who—stands on the boat with one hand out holding the mast just under the lighted bell eggs on the insect swarm of terror within. It all comes as a rush of blasting cold across my skin. My knees lock.

My head swivels every way, searching for an easy out. But standing in this vulnerable clearing, with the mangroves behind and the river and manned boat ahead, a fast escape is nonexistent. The sight of this demonic figure strikes fear directly into my spine like a botched epidural zinging electricity to the tips of my digits.

I shouldn't run. Hell, I can't run.

My body is frozen from the chilling grasp upon my spine. The figure steps from boat to shore and begins closing the distance between us. He moves with a sort of hallowed grace, which does not at all match his dark aesthetic. The echoes of his armored boots clunk heavily and with purpose against the stone. A long cloak drapes around him down to the ground, and the large hood he wears hangs loosely from atop his forehead to almost halfway down his back. Most noticeable however—the gunmetal-toned blindfold strapped from ear to ear, completely covering where eyes would normally be, and the massively wide-open smile stretching fully across his face.

His strides halt just a few paces from me. He goes completely inanimate and simply stands there with the massive toothy smile he wears that seems permanent. My knees are still locked, even faintly shaking now. Insects continue their plague, though I begin to envy the appearance of this monster. He's dark, strong, nightmarish—all of which are qualities I wish were my own.

Standing this close brings me much more detail of whatever this monstrosity is. The metal or shiny stone blindfold he wears doesn't seem to be worn at all, but rather looks to be surgically installed. Scar tissue around the edges gives the look that it's embedded into his face. In some sections, his pale dirty flesh has started to grow up onto the serpent scales that pattern the blindfold. This large scaled pattern matches his other armored adornments, such as his greaves and gauntlets.

His grin gets somehow even taller and wider as he says, "Where to?"

His words and face do not move with the grace of his walk. Instead, he speaks and moves his intense grin sharply in jarring fast movements, tilting his head slightly after offering his question.

A mass grows in my throat; beads form at my brow; and my words come out choked and stammered. I force them through after a difficult swallow. "Uh, I—I'm not sure I have a destination. Rather, I'm-m-m more interested in understanding where I currently am." I give a slight pause. I can't help but peek again to my right. *Gah, nope, no escape.* "What is this place?"

Again, he's still, inanimate, never losing his sinister grin. I am in disbelief. Surely the towering void of teeth—fangs, even— couldn't take up any more of his face. There's almost no face at all, but rather an endless ominous maw and the metal blindfold, which I assume renders the demonic being completely blind.

Jerking his head back straight, he snaps, "What name does thou bare?" again ending with a sudden tilt of his head.

He's asking my name, right? "I do not know my name," I say. "Nor anything of my past, really." I feel foolish. *Do I really not even know my damn name?*

Keeping his head tilted, he slowly raises his armored hand, eventually straightening an unimaginably long and sharp index finger at the center of my head.

"You . . . not supposed be here."

This time, his mouth closes with a loud tooth-on-tooth smash of bone. His smile shuts with purpose and is gone as instantly as he finishes his statement. I tremble slightly, shaking at the way the grand maw of teeth slowly expands back into a grin of horror.

"What payment you possess?" he spits. "What coin have you?"

Bringing out the two gold coins, I present them in an open yet tremoring hand. "These are my only possessions. I do not know how I came about them."

His head jerks, tilting now to the other side. "Truth coins," he utters lowly. "Everyone choices to be good. Everyone choices to be bad. That's the truth, ha! I cannot take these as payment. Other types of coins are gifted to those upon the falling. Thou are supposed to know thine name, however." His throat rattles gravelly in contemplation. "This may be why you have no other coin. Yes . . . this why. You not supposed be here," he concludes in his low stone grating voice.

I am feeling even more lost and confused than before. Nothing this monstrosity says makes any damn sense. He's only bringing more questions to my mind, and his broken speech does *not* help in the least.

"Yeah, well, I agree. I don't think I'm supposed to be here either. I have no idea where I am or what this damned place is! Or who or what you are, for that matter," I bark almost more than say.

The monstrosity straightens his head again, opening his maw even wider than previously witnessed, and lets out a single, "Ha!" And again, he instantly closes his toothy grin with a sundering audible smash.

"I am the boatman, Doom's Mariner. I am Karhon of the Rivers." He pauses and bows his tilted head to me, all the while still seemingly watching me with his forsaken maw. "And you are at the Deliverance Gates of the End Realm."

"End Realm?" I question.

"Ha!" he responds, again with what seems to be his usual desire to deafen me with his jaw snapping shut. The concussive smashing of his massive teeth is felt deep in my bones.

"Realm of the Dead, the underworld, heaven, hell, choose your title—that is your current position, my soulless lost one."

"Wait," I say with a chuckle. "You're saying I'm *dead*? And this is hell?"

"Thou are in the End Realm. Thou are as dead as the dead," he says, grinning. He points at me again with his grim and assaulting finger. "Not supposed be here. Thine memories and name should have followed you through the falling."

"I don't understand. How does—"

"And this is not hell!" he blasts. "There is no separate heaven and hell. Only the End Realm."

"Ooo-kay . . ." I drag out. "But I don't understand. How have I gotten here without memories? And why am I soulless, as you say?"

"Sinners not grateful for their own gift of life above, abusers and killers of the innocent—the list goes on, but these are the *usual* ones who end up soulless in the realm. I call you soulless because you have no coin and are therefore bound for Tartarus. You have truth coins though." Again, his smile goes as wide and tall as it can. "That, I not seen *ever*."

"What are these coins used for?"

"Used in rituals, traded at times, but most powerful use is to exchange for answers and information from the Devil-God Hades or the arch-sorceress. Cannot seek an audience with Hades, however. Only summoned can thou be. The truth coins, they rare."

"You've never seen truth coins before this, boatman?"

"Ha!" He laughs, with the usual slam of his jaw. "Say me as Karhon," he says as he bows his tilted head to me again. "Seen truth coins, yes, yet rare. Heard of them being used, rarer yet! What haven't seen is a soulless with any coin other than Tartarus coins. As that's their permittance and the only area I therefore take them."

"All right, where can you take me, then? I'm lost and confused, even with the information you have given. I'm guessing the best thing for me right now is to find my soul somehow? And find answers about my past, regain lost memories, and maybe then I will understand better how I've found myself here."

Karhon remains inanimate for what seems an awkwardly long time.

"Firstly," he says. "You not need find your soul. *Soulless* is just what walkers bound for Tartarus are called since they're usually nasty beings and deserve the prisons. Lastly, with the lack of coin you possess, I can only take thou to the lowest prison in Tartarus. Soulless without a Tartarus coin can stand no trial, and therefore, they must remain in the lowest prison, never to leave.

"You see, you have rarest coin. Yes, the truth coin, but they used only for answers and rituals. They not grant access to an area of the realm. With no other coin"—he shakes his head—"your soul is permitted only to the Lowest, which is lowest and worst of prisons in Tartarus."

I begin laughing. "Well, fuck. I'll just stay here on my own and attempt to better my situation myself, then. Surely that sounds better than going to a prison."

Karhon's demonic grin sinks a little, and though still remaining a smile, it somehow looks to go a bit sullen and sad. "I can only take thou to the Lowest," he says again, pausing a moment after. "I am Doom's Mariner. I under Hades command, the command to direct and distribute the walkers entering this realm. Want to help as much I can, but there is no escape from me. I *plead* with you not to run, my soulless one."

As I hear all this, my heart—or where my heart should be (do I even have a heart right now?)—sinks and goes empty and cold. I do not fear Karhon any longer, but I can also tell that if I attempt to evade and get in the way of this demon doing his job, things will quickly go severely bad for me. Judging the monstrosity's demeanor and physical attributes, I have no reason to doubt that Karhon could kill and devour me with that unholy maw in the most gruesome of ways, even if he desired not to.

I sigh deep and heavily.

"Is there anything else you can aid me in before I am ferried to this . . . prison? Can you offer any more useful information or advice to me?"

Karhon solemnly bows his tilted head and grotesque grin. "I may not say it advice, but do not ever lose or barter thy truth coins, my soulless one. They rare. Trust no one in Tartarus. Place is filled with scum, traitors. And I hope thee finds one's memories and name. Wish for thou to find the answers thou seeks, yet I only know of two who could possibly offer the truths—one being Hades himself and other, thy arch-sorceress, Lunacrye. She is in the High Sanctum near the Fields of Asphodel. You will never meet her though as soulless prisoner."

Karhon's smile seems to go sad again, like he has realized there's no hope for me. Noticing this, I feel vanquished from within and now not only lost, but also helpless. I raise my hand, gesturing to speak again, but he raises his armored palm faster and stops me with his raspy dark voice.

"Aboard now, my soulless one. I must take thou."

CHAPTER TWO

Gifts

S ilence falls upon the ferry for what seems like hours.
Karhon sits at the front of the boat holding one hand on
the dimly lit mast, and somehow, the hanging bell is silent
even as it wavers, as if its chime was never from movement, but
some other magical source. The rear of the boat has been my
place, a mere couple paces from the front, where Karhon has
remained, facing forward, directing us without oars of any kind.

The river we travel is a thin winding path that holds the very
darkness of the new world I find myself in. Closely resembling
the sky above, the slow rippleless yet churning liquid has what
look like flakes of silver suspended throughout its seemingly
endless depths. It makes me think of the night sky from the
living world I have knowledge of—a night sky filled with stars
of silver light spread across deeply pooled ink. We pass small
shores and more dense areas of leafless foliage of all heights and
sizes. My eyes constantly make their way back to the river. I find
it beautiful, mesmerizing, and . . . nostalgic somehow. It feels
impossible to not gaze into its eternity, losing myself within its
depths. The river steals my worry. It casts my confusion away. It
makes me feel safely at home, away from the otherwise plagued
and lost state I've found myself in since my arrival here.

13

"It's a long trip. No point in a hurry though."

As Karhon's cold gritty voice breaks the long silence, I still remain in the silver stars of the abyssal river.

"At times, she is kind enough to force gifts unto the walkers," he continues.

Realizing after a few seconds that I can't make sense of the boatman's latest broken rambling, I reluctantly point my chin his way, my eyes trailing behind, not wanting to lose the dreamy view.

"Who is this now?" I ask.

"The river, my soulless one. She, at times, will bear gifts."

"I don't really get what you're saying, Karhon. Sorry."

With the back of his hood still facing me, Karhon goes on. "Thou can continue to stare her way or you can offer her a hand to meet. Thou choices are thy own. Choices . . . Ha!" He laughs, and his maw collapses, bone meeting bone. "Choices we make. Choices make us. Our souls are the sum of choices."

I blankly stare ahead. Not that I am entranced by the back of the boatman's cloak, but rather, I become infatuated with his statement. I have no personal recollection of my life's choices, but I do understand and believe that our choices make us who we are. Now, everyone makes choices they themselves may regret or deem bad, but they can also choose to make future choices. Future choices based on growth, growth of their morality and themselves. Their ever-evolving morality is their own after all and may even fairly contradict and oppose another's. *This possibly blurs the line between good and evil to some degree . . . Hmm.* Thinking of all the caveats to this, I find its complexity enthralling! *I wonder what the sum of my choices has made me.*

I blink and bring myself out of that deep mental trance.

"I find truth in that, Karhon," I say, tilting my own head a bit. "I agree."

I gaze back down at the river and again catch myself in awe at its appearance as well as the effect it has on my emotions. I can't quite explain or describe the exact feeling, but it's familiar, nostalgic, and clear in a way that makes me feel close to a distant memory or maybe another person or entity even. I don't feel so lost or, more importantly, alone when viewing the obsidian waters and silver flakes of these timeless stars.

What Karhon said about the river giving gifts plays through my mind. In his aberrant way of speech, he made it sound as though the river is alive or sentient somehow and . . . female?

"Karhon, does this river have a name?"

"Ah, yes. She takes the name Styx, soulless one."

I feel no danger from the depths on which we ride. Quite the opposite, in fact. I offer her my hand. The liquid of the river is surprisingly viscous and slightly warmer than the cool but comfortable ambient air. As suspended flakes find themselves colliding with my palm and fingers, I feel increasingly less alone. Some pass through my fingers, while others skip across as they barely catch contact with my skin.

Wow, so surreal. My hand begins to collect more and more starry flakes as a number of them collide and stick. I rush my hand in violent movements through the viscous river to lose the attached silver and start again with a clean flesh colored hand. I do this over and over. It's no longer just me in the back of the boat; it's me and the flakes. I am no longer lost and alone.

I take notice that my hand seems to become engulfed in silver quicker each time I shake them away back into the depths. The flakes gain haste, as if they're attracted to me now. Shaking and waving my hand through the river only entices them more and more, like I am being homed in on and chased. My breath suddenly goes shallow, and a knot grips inside my stomach. *Eh, not liking this.* I start withdrawing my hand from the dark liquid. Instead, I am thrust farther into the water as if something has grabbed my entire hand and wrist and drags me into the ink all the way past my elbow. I am damn near pulled all the way in, and if not for quickly grabbing the side of the boat with my other hand and bracing my knees against the edge of the craft, I don't doubt that Karhon would've had to pull me out of the river himself. I shoot up a look to Karhon, my eyes asking, pleading for help. For the first time in more than half a day, the boatman's not facing forward, but rather, his towering grin meets my desperate gaze.

"Help! It has my arm!"

The boatman stares, remaining in his common inanimate state.

"Karhon!" I scream, giving him the neediest and most terrified look I am capable of. Fear grips my spine again with its chilling grasp as it did when I first met the boatman. The cold rushes through me, reaching the center of my bones, and bumps crawl across my skin. I heave at my arm again, again, again.

"I *beg* you, Karhon! The river fucking has me, damn it! Fuck!" I bark in resignation.

I am met with null but the blank stare from his impenetrable blindfold and massive demonic maw stuck in the most haunting ominous smile imaginable. This time, the sinister smile has something different about it, something barely hidden—a hint of intrigue and plotted excitement. Karhon is still, inanimate. I do not even think the demon ever has to breathe.

I look back at the water pulling down on my arm. My continued attempts to wrench myself free from the invisible grasp fail. Not only my hand, but up to my elbow just below where the black water's grip begins is now completely enameled in silver. The silver flakes have created an armor of starlight, and the weight of the armor aids the river in its meal. My arm becomes harder and harder to budge in the tug-of-war and seems to keep increasing in weight, making it difficult to tell if I am still being pulled in by some unknown force or if I am simply a ship's anchor now, begging for the river's floor.

Out of nowhere, momentum suddenly changes. The black abyss stops churning; the wind ceases; and the boat, instead of bobbing and weaving with the water, has come to a complete halt. My silver-clad arm stuck in the river is now solid as stone.

Though the rest of my body is free to move, everything else sits in strange and frightening stillness.

Karhon is gone, having seemingly disappeared. It's as if I've instantly transferred to a different plane. I brace myself against the craft, square my shoulders, and give another mighty heave at my arm stuck in the frozen stillness of the river. Shards of black fly everywhere as my arm jolts and shatters free. The crystalline shards of the solid river move in slow motion all around me as they explode from where my arm was held. Then they become still, suspended in the atmosphere all around me. A jagged crater now lies in the river where my arm was cemented, resembling the aftermath of a mortar strike. The resulting shrapnel of black material speckled with silver flakes suspends in air all around.

I can now move my arm some but only in slow motion, the heavy weight of it dragging. Then even that promise stops. I lose control of my body and instantly become suspended in anima-tion myself. Frozen, I can do nothing but watch as a slashing ray of white light streaks in front of me and severs my silver hand from my forearm right at the wrist. My armored hand falls slowly through the thick air that seems to slow everything and stops midair a short time after just as the black shards did moments ago. I feel no physical pain from the butchering, just intense horror as blood starts to ooze out of the wound across my wrist and too my detached floating hand.

This can't be happening. Get me out. I want goddamned out of this!

The inside of my skull becomes consumed; I am freaking out. All control is lost, all control over my own actions and body, my emotions and thought processes. I can barely breath, feeling as though I am close to hyperventilating. I am drifting into shock and on the border of losing consciousness. It is all just too much to handle mentally. My brain is on the brink of overload and about to give up on me.

Blood continues pooling out of my wounds and floats in a wobbling fashion in front of me, as if there is no gravity to force it in any specific direction. A spinning object catches me as it comes into my stationary field of view. Rising up to the five-digit clad-in-silver hand, its spin begins to slow. The object is a ring made of deep bronze or some other dark metallic material or element. I watch as the ring travels its way around pooling globs of suspended blood, up and around the palm, and then down the length of the fourth finger, ending its tranquilly slow journey down at the base of the starlit digit.

My vision starts to go . . . funny. The world around me looks to vibrate and shake with acceleration, but I can tell it's trickery in my eyes and not the world ahead of me truly quaking. Quickly, it increases to a point where I can't discern anything. All that's seen is a shaking jumble of mixed noise consisting of the colors and contrasts of the realm.

A heavy kick boulders my chest. It feels as if a huge anvil were dropped on me. I feel crushed under the immense con-cussive weight. At the same time, my corrupted vision reaches pitch-black, turning then to the previous state of dizzying noise and that then giving way soon to clear sight. Clear sight of the weaving boat, moving waters of the river, and the intact anatomy of my human flesh-colored hand and arm. Looking up from my now fashioned finger, I meet Karhon's stare.

"Well, what did thou get?" he asks with a previously unseen and heard enthusiasm.

I raise my left hand. "A ring." I glare. "Something cut my fucking hand off just to put this goddamn ring on my finger!"

Catching myself, I realize my tone's turned to growling loudly at Karhon, and this may not be the wisest conduct to direct his way. Sighing, I sit back a bit and slouch some in an attempt to show a more settled and maybe apologetic demeanor.

"Aye, she finds a way to blood. She needs taste of one's blood to surely identify and offer a correct gift and to the correct owner."

I sit there for moments, gathering myself and just taking time to breathe. And trying to find a feeling of reality as the feeling of dream and nightmare has hit an overwhelming state. Looking away and off over the shore to my left in the distance, I say, "That's—I mean, this is all really fucked up. On an unfathomable level."

My words are met with silence. I look back to Karhon. He's now faced ahead again, watching in the direction of travel. I guess watching? I can't help but laugh inside. What the hell *is* he doing? Smiling blindly at the way ahead? Just the idea of the boatman directing his insane smile and solid stonelike blindfold any particular direction comes to me as asinine, to the point that I struggle. It's difficult for me to not laugh audibly. There is no doubt—an incredibly good chance indeed—that my current mental state and previous circumstances play a role in my current off-pitch sense of humor. Basically, I'm losing it. This is all too much.

After taking some time to catch myself, I am able to process and think more about this ring I've procured. I have the knowledge to understand a ring on one's left fourth finger is where people wear their rings of wedlock—wedlock rings being jewelry exchanged at spousal ceremonies as a symbol of their declaration of everlasting love, loyalty, and faithfulness to the other person, the pairing, and relationship the two people share. This strikes me. This is a big deal to me. I know not of who I am wedded to, but I know such significant vows are extremely important to me and my character. I peer out over the river into the fogged near-blackened line of trees. *If it's true, I wonder your name, your face, your sex . . .* I sigh.

I wonder where you are.

"Halfway, my soulless one. Halfway," Karhon interrupts my train of thought.

I don't offer Karhon a response, but I am taken aback by how long of a journey it is to this Tartarus place. I am grateful, however, as I can't imagine the hell prison I am on my way to would be better than my current situation in any possible way.

I am in no hurry to get off this boat, boatman.

CHAPTER THREE

Gifts (Continued...)

T he landscape is starting to change drastically. Trees are now eight stories high or higher, creating a canopy so thick that the endless sky of blank darkness now goes unseen. The height of the trees together with the atmosphere in this realm being so dark makes it so I cannot tell if these new trees are bare and leafless like the foliage of yesterday or not. Their closely together trunks reaching straight up and only branching out at the canopy level, too high in the distance for my eyes to discern any detail. Rolling sections of stone ground became more and more sparse, giving way to the sharp jagged landscape that appears to be impossible to traverse at no risk.

The realm has been vacant. Other than Karhon and myself, the afterlife so far seems to be a land of my own. I've seen no other humans—or "walkers," as Karhon has labeled them several times—and I've spotted no other forms of life other than the different species of trees. I am spending a lot of time in my head; this is almost forced upon me though, as the boatman offers no more conversation, and the last attempt on my part by asking how much longer we had until we reached the prison was met with his silent stare down the river.

A long time has been spent overthinking the possibilities of the river's gift to me. And I contemplate many aspects of this. Is it even a ring of wedlock? There is always the possibility that I just wore a ring on this finger for another reason. Maybe simply because I preferred how it looked or felt on that finger instead of others. I feel the chances of this are low, however, simply because in the living world, I know wearing a ring on the fourth finger is globally known as a sign of spousal union. I also find myself wondering where my partner is. Are they here, in the End Realm? Are they still in the living world without me? If the person is dead, could I find them here? Even if they are dead though, I am on my path to Tartarus, which Karhon made pretty clear there was no escaping from. My unknown partner is also just that—unknown. I know not their name, their origin, or anything of their appearance. I know nothing of them. How do you find someone you know absolutely nothing of? You don't.

Quite frankly, I could end up sharing a prison cell with my beloved and I wouldn't know the difference. What makes this all even more difficult to grasp and think about on a logical level is the feeling of failure, and in a certain way, my betrayal lingers over me, weighting me down as if I have something emotionally crushing my chest and fogging my brain with anxious waves. It becomes clear to me that disloyalty, dishonor, unfaithfulness, disrespect, and letting down anyone who is a loved one or dear friend of mine are simply not options for me. This is where this almost crippling feeling of failure birthed from, I believe. If someone was promised that I would always be there for them, if someone relied on me and trusted I was to be their shadow, by their side whenever wanted or needed, and here I am on the barge of hell, completely incapable of fulfilling any of those oaths I made . . . Just the possibility of that encumbers me with a grave feeling of failure. I know nothing of myself or my past; it's become clear though that being loyal and devout is not only important to me, but is something rooted into my very being. It is who and what I am.

As the abyssal starlit river holds my gaze, I realize more than one gift came my way. A ring, yes, but with it, an understanding—a glimpse of who I am and what some of my governing characteristics are. At this point at least, learning this little piece about myself feels more a gift than the tangible dark bronze ring embellishing my left hand. Silently, I speak a word of thanks to the river. The gratitude is sincere and genuine but undoubtedly goes unheard, I am sure.

"Soulless one, we are here. These are thy gates."

Peeling myself from the river once more, eyes trailing behind, my mouth slackens, and my jaw drops. I am appalled by the site of "my gates," as Karhon puts it. It looks as though another five-minute journey will have me right under this colossal wall ahead. Like the first wall I saw, the verticality is never-ending. The door this time though is instead a barred gate that oddly enough has large gaps in between the massive crosshatched rods, making escape appear easy . . . if it wasn't for the seemingly stone-still army in front and on either side of the prison's entrance. I assume it's a real army and not mere statues like they appear from this distance though, because several hundred statues in echelon infantry formation, well, that just doesn't make any damn sense.

"What is the larger figure front and center, Karhon?"

I wish Karhon would stop getting increasingly reticent. I am again met with his silence.

"Come on, Karhon. Please talk with me," I say. "If I'm being vulnerable, I'm beside myself. I'm . . . I'm fucking scared, man."

Still, silence.

I sit back down, resting my palms against my forehead. "I don't know what's to come ahead. I don't know what this all means." *This is it, isn't it? From this point on, endless days in prison, in hell.* My fingers spread through my hair, taking grip at my scalp.

He doesn't turn around, but I hear him while my eyes stare into the wood at my feet.

"Alastor of Chains," Karhon says. "He is the chief warden, appointed by Hades himself centuries ago when he ripped Gabriel's wings off. See, Alastor witnessed Gabriel, who was the chief warden at the time, abandon his post. Alastor saw the butchering a fit discipline."

Not having anything to really say to that, I ask, even though the answer chisels at my ear, "Will he be the one taking me?" A hard swallow drums in my throat.

"I am to deliver thou, yes, soulless one."

"What can I expect up here? What's to happen once we part ways?"

Again, I find myself met with the still view of the boatman's hood and damning silence as he remains faced away toward the destination.

I sit back and find my breath shortening. Wet pills bead my brow while my face flushes a richer warmer hue. As we get closer, I make out more of the stature and composition of both the wall of Tartarus and the warden. The wall I previously thought to be inlaid with ornate designs is not that at all. We are close enough now to see that the rusted iron-colored prison wall is built of bodies. Human, animal, and other corporeal figures I do not recognize from the living world are piled and twisted amongst one another in every direction. The corpses do not look to be in any state of decay, though they're all twisted and smashed together in mass disorder and shine in rusted deep reds and orange tinges against a lead base.

I know not for certain if the wall is composed of once living flesh or if the corpses were sculpted from ore; however, my gut sides with the former. The gory sight does not aid in reducing the hold fear has on me, and I have a suspicion that the macabre architecture and murderous-looking infantry line ahead are honest signs of what world I am to soon enter.

The warden stands taller than the line soldiers, most of their heads meeting his enameled breast plate, his shoulders towering over them. The only armor the warden wears is a solid chest plate, gauntlets, and a single left pauldron. The chromed armor contrasts brightly against the dark twisting horns escaping his skull and his ashen coat. The demon's tall stature makes his legs prominently stand out; they are built of several more joints than I am accustomed to seeing on a biped. This includes a large hock where, proportionately, you would typically find a human's knee. This and his coat are not his only equine looking features. He doesn't bear the full snout a horse would have, but overall, the warden's face much resembles that of one. His demonic figure is not hulking yet supremely sinister-looking, exuding power where he stands. As I do not doubt that Karhon could gruesomely ravage my body with his evil maw, I have no reservations that the horse demon, Alastor, could take off my head with a single swipe of his hand.

The boat stops its forward advance, and the boatman, blinded by the serpent scaled visor across his face, stares at me hauntingly with his towering teeth and vast smile.

"My soulless one," Karhon starts in an almost grief-stricken manner. "Before we meet the shore, I desire to offer thou two things."

"I'm fucking scared, man. I—I really don't want to go. What's going to happen to me up there?" My voice quivers under itself. "And beyond that . . . in the prison?"

Moments pass as we sit in the still boat with no further exchange. Karhon becomes inanimate as he does, with his elbows rested on his knees as he sits opposite me. His sharp armored hands fold into each other in front of him, and he slouches forward a bit, with his head in a slight tilt, gazing at me through his ominously dour grin.

"I desire to part ways with mine oldest and first weapon, acquired to me so far long in the past I not have memory of its beginning."

Looking down, he grasps the inner side of his left greave, and with a sound of strong sturdy metal wracking apart, the full inside of his upper greave snaps away. As he holds the separated portion of his armor out to me, I can distinguish that a handle and deep red jeweled pommel the color of coagulated blood extrudes from the piece of armor that once completed the boatman's greave. I lean forward and take the short section of armor that now acts solely as a stow and sheath for the large dagger I pull from it. The weapon is beautiful. The blade looks to be crafted of solid onyx rather than steel and is quite wide for a dagger. The hilt and pommel appear to be crafted of two different metals, both a slightly different shade of gray than the other and twisted together, which I guess to be the result of a folding technique blacksmiths use to create extra durability in their weaponry.

"The jewel—I been told the throne of Hades has a single empty setting on its facing about the same size. Just stories though," Karhon says low and gravelly. "A blood jewel it is named. New deposits have not been found in ages."

The single jewel can be seen from both sides and is set in the center of the pommel. It's not faceted. Instead, it looks to be in its raw and discovered form. Though it's not a shiny or vibrant gem, I still find it rewarding to look at. Somehow, when turned and seen from different angles, the inside of the gem seems to move, as if the jewel is a vessel for another nonsolid substance.

"This is a beautiful gift, Karhon, but am I able to possess this in Tartarus?"

"Ha! Yes," he shoots back in a way that makes my question feel humorous and absurd.

"I feel less small and meek now having this. Thank you, boatman."

"My hope is that it cares for thou, as thou cares for it."

"I don't really know what to say. I feel at a loss for words, and also, I am not sure I understand the reason for such friendly benefaction. You've given me something that requires you losing a piece of your armor, and it is so old not even you know its legacy. What have I done to deserve such a thing? And more importantly, how can I repay you?"

Karhon, smiling of course in his sinister way, reaches out his hand armored in sharp serpentine plates and gazes blindly my way. "As the second, I most desire to offer thou mine hand."

As vexatious as it has been having Karhon disregard certain questions and avenues of communication I've posed, I have quickly learned that just because I ask, does not mean I am to receive an answer or even an acknowledgment.

With his hand out, the boatman bows his head. I reach out, honored at the opportunity, and meet his hand with mine as firmly as I can. Meeting Karhon's hand and attempting so in a firm and strong manner proves difficult, as my hand is easily lost in the mass of the monster's. His clawlike long fingers and palm are at least twice mine in size. As the motionless handshake continues for a moment, I find myself yearning to stay with the monstrous demon—even if it means staying on the boat in silence. Having no memory of anyone else, having no companions of any kind, and the boatman being the only living thing I've encountered thus far has me wishing not to let go of it all, his hand included. In a way, I somehow see Karhon of the Rivers as a friend.

The boat begins to continue its way to the shore, where the warden awaits my arrival. Karhon drops his hand back to the other in the same folded fashion as before, and we make our way to the shoreline, with Karhon never un-bowing his head and another word never being spoken.

CHAPTER FOUR

Branded

R ed dust spins off the sandstone floor and whips through the air in smooth raging currents. A salted rank smell of dense animal fur catches in one and hits my nose, telling me I am far closer than I wish.

"Fresh soulless," Alastor barks in a low guttural tone. "Show the coin you bring. Is it Tartarus or is it Lowest?"

His heavy hooves clop the rusted sandstone as he steps forward. Warm breaths heave down on me. He is tall, taller than Karhon even. I do not dare to look up or withdraw the hand shielding my eyes from the red dust currents. The smell of warm animal breath chokes my attempts to find a gust of fresh air.

"I have none," I yell through the winds.

"Roumph!" the horse demon growls. "I won't ask again, fowl creature. Without a Tartarus coin, you won't have a trial with the council, you won't choose your circle, and you shall be cast to the Lowest. Now, show it!"

I need to heed Karhon's words. I don't want anyone knowing about or stealing the truth coins. I don't even want to tell the warden. "I have none to show," I yell. "But the boatman said this is where he must take me."

Alastor chortles, his breaths now sharper and heavier against me as he brings his head down closer to mine. "Then it is to the Lowest for you, scum," he says so only I can hear.

"Rahkni, bind his hand," Alastor barks.

The hand shielding my eyes is forced down by a tight grip. My eyes are blasted with the red sandy mixture being swung through the air. A dark gray feathered figure has control of my arm. They look muscular and mostly human, though feathers and gray down coat their entire body. Large jet-black iridescent wings unfurl away from their back and block the rushing air currents from reaching me now. Alastor steps forward, and the dark angel figure pulls my arm taut toward the warden and cinches their grip even tighter around my wrist. Alastor hovers his hand above mine and starts tracing symbols in the air. The air glows golden with each symbol completed. He pauses and looks down at me. Our eyes meet for the first time.

"Here is your brand, foul creature from above. Welcome to Tartarus. Welcome to hell."

The golden glow within the air from the traced symbols is sucked into a single point. The point is Alastor's claw, and it suddenly glows red—ember hot. The top of my hand can feel the radiant heat even though the warden's hand still hovers well above my own. The warden chortles again as he starts to trace red lines in the air. I feel searing pain rip across the thin flesh on the back of my hand. The burn matches the red etchings Alastor creates. I look from his claw down to my hand that is tightly held in place by the dark angel, Rahkni. Searing lines of boiling scar tissue rise on my hand as the horse demon finishes his tracing spell, laughing.

I try to pull my arm away from the hellfire, but the angel is far too strong. He has me bound. It does not matter how much extra strength the pain bestows on me; there is no escape for my hand. I assail the red dust storm around us with pleading screams. My throat starts to tear itself raw. My vision goes white. My knees crash against the sandstone.

"Drag this one in," Alastor barks. "And take him deep!" His hooves retreat, and a sudden break from the smell of fur wafts across my face.

I am pulled by my arms, feet dragging behind while I try to catch my legs up to the rest of me. My vision is still flashes of white with vague outlines, and my hand throbs in horrific metronome. Hours must go by. The reddened landscape turns to a tint of yellow, becoming even more barren. The scent of sulfur ignites my nostrils, permeating deep enough to reach back behind my eyes, stinging. The entourage of guard escorts dwindles the farther in we go until only two remain, pushing me forward, giving jabs with spears or grunting in frustration when my pace displeases them.

I expected a descent by now, though nothing but flat barren sulfuric wasteland has come forth and been put behind us. My attention is grabbed at times by stone or sometimes brick buildings. Walkers near them or just inside sometimes peer out through the sediment-polluted air at me, though none get too close. Most are wearing ragged torn clothing, often with a kerchief or scarf over their nose and mouth.

Fucking wish I had something of my own to filter this trash air . . .

"How much farth—"

A heavy blow attacks the back of my knee, and it gives out like a wet rag. I drop like dead weight. My knee hits the yellowed cracked desert and shatters the plate of stone beneath like it's nothing but crunchy baked mud. "Farther now that you thought yourself worthy of speaking directly to one of the Chain's guards," the guard to my left says.

"Ah, frak. Come on, Jarr," the other protests. "We're already within the ninth gap. Let's just chuck him in the next box and be done with him. Look, there's one right up here." This one's voice is high-pitched and strained, sounding as though they are not human, or if they are, they suffered some severe neck or vocal injury.

Taking me by the upper arm, they usher me briskly over to one of the buildings, the cased opening on this one half fallen in on itself, the rubble strewn about the archway.

"Aye! Chain guard here," the high-pitched one yells in. "How many?"

"Just one." The male voice thinly rides from the shadow of the chamber.

The guard at my arm snickers. "Yeah, that's all I need to hear." He grips tighter, pushing me forward, and shoves me off hard through the cased opening. I nearly trip as my right foot catches on one of the larger fallen archway rocks; I'm surprised I keep afoot, albeit ungracefully. I glance back through the opening. The two guards' backs show stowed spears as they fade away through the sulfuric haze.

"Not going to lie, been ages since I've had a cell mate," says the voice from the far shadowed corner. He stands and slaps his hands across each other, dusting them off. Blue flames flicker across his figure from the magical-looking fire pit between us. He wears goggles stowed on his forehead and a kerchief loosely below his chin. As he walks round toward me, he continues, "And to not lie again, not entirely sure how I feel about it, but the name's Cerutam." He extends a hand. I meet it firmly—and wince. "Ah, sure. A fresh brand hurts like hell, doesn't it, man?" He laughs a bit. "It *does* get better, but man . . . it doesn't go away. I've been here, well, *too* long—let's just leave it at that for now—and I still get ghost pains every once in a while."

"You're human?"

"Yeah. Hard to tell some of the walker species apart, I know. But yeah, I'm human. Most of us are, here in the Lowest, I mean, not a surprise though, right? Humans are so damn greedy and disgusting. It's almost as if this place were made just for us alone." He laughs a bit more and retreats back to the corner of the shelter from which he came. "So what's your name, man?"

I follow suit and sit down. The cracked desert floor offers less comfort than I wish for. "Don't have a name."

He scoffs. "Ah, you're going to be like that, huh? Listen, this isn't like the prisons from the living world. We don't need to lie about our names or insist on our innocence. There's just no reason to. Up there in the living world, there may be reason to hold on to facades and hope, but down here, man, there's no escape, and there's no reason to pretend. Because this shit's forever."

I hold my branded hand at the wrist, squeezing with some pressure—just instinct kicking in to try to deal with the hellfire searing across in waves. "Nah, I really mean it. Well, I guess more accurately, I don't *know* my name. I'm sure I have one—or had one, rather. But yeah, no idea what the fuck my name is and no idea who the hell I was. My memory has pretty much been wiped apparently."

"Hrmm." He eyes me, searching for insight. Pulls his goggles down over his eyes, peering deeper in search. The blue flames refract in a dance on the scratched and dusty lenses. He slides the goggles back to rest on his forehead. "Well, I can't say I've ever heard of that happening, but stranger things have happened, I suppose. So, if you say so, man."

"So, what's it like down here?"

"What's it like down here?" he mocks, laughing. "This. This is what it's like, man." He gestures around at the walls encompassing us, the magical fire pit, the archway, and beyond. "Eternity in this flat wasted land. It's like what you see, man. What you saw on your walk in and what ya see in our cell here. Not much else to it."

"The boatman made it sound like, well, worse or something, I guess."

"Well, this place is damned terrible. Trust me on that! And there are dangers to always keep an eye open for, but uh—wait, the boatman spoke to you?" Cerutam asks with a raised brow.

"I mean, yeah. Yeah, we talked some. There were definitely times when a question I posed was met with silence and him doing that creepy-as-fuck thing where he stands still as a statue, but he told me a bit about Tartarus and the black river." I hold up my left hand. "The damn river sent me to this dreamlike place and cut off my damn hand while I was there. Saw the whole thing happen in front of me but could do nothing. Then this ring came out of nowhere and floated around, then down my finger. I think it's a ring of wedlo—"

"Now you're starting to piss me off, man." Cerutam stands and points at me, shaking his finger like he doesn't know what to do. He walks around the fire pit to me, shoulders and head leading the way. "Let me see it!"

I abruptly stand, half-prepared to defend myself. "Would you fucking chill?" I say. "Don't get pissed at me. I didn't ask for any of this." I show him the ring on my finger. "I think it's a ring of wedlock. It's the only thing that makes sense to me. Don't know for certain though since I can't remember a fucking thing from before the gates."

Cerutam grabs my hand and inspects the ring from a close and personal three inches away. He brings his goggles down again and gets even closer, the lenses damn near hitting the jewelry.

"All right, all right, jeesh," I say, pulling my hand away. "It's just a ring, man. Chill. And what do those goggles do, by the way?"

"*Do?* Ack, they don't do anything. It's always worth a shot though." He stows his goggles and starts scratching his chin.

Yup. This asshole's not all there.

"How do I know you didn't enter the realm *with* the ring, huh? Prove to me you got it as you say you did."

"How the hell do you expect me to do that? And what's it matter if I got it from the river or if I came here with it? Listen,

I've had a fucking horrible time so far. This being dead thing? Yeah, so far, not a good gig. So I need you to just back the fuck off a bit and chill."

His fingernails continue scratching, making the sound of sandpaper. Then he stops and points. "What's that?"

Ah, shit . . .

"I came here with that," I lie.

"No. No ya didn't. Never seen anything in here as nice as that, man. Now, where did you get it?"

He isn't going to let it go. Damn it.

"The boatman gave it to me, said he wanted me to have it. He also said if anyone but me wields it, he will know—instantly." *This is the one thing that gives me any sense of safety here. No one's touching the dagger.*

"Nope. Nope, this isn't right." He's shaking his head. "This stuff doesn't happen, man. The Maw doesn't lend weapons, and the river doesn't give gifts. I've been here for over a thousand earth years. A thousand." His finger jabs hard against his chest. "And this kind of thing doesn't happen. Here, you wanna see what the boatman—the Maw—does? Come on, I'll show you," he says as he heads toward the cased opening. "Come on, man, won't take long. I'll show you some stuff. And hide that dagger of yours. You don't want other walkers knowing you have that."

He disappears into the yellow tinted haze.

Gah, not back out there in that shitstorm. I really need one of those damn kerchiefs.

I follow.

We venture forth into the wastes of the Lowest. I keep up with my cell mate as best I can while my eyes and nostrils erupt in irritation from the acrid fumes. Cerutam seems to be on the chase for something, changing directions often and taking us within viewing distance of other shelters at times, then darting off through the winds and haze, leaving me each time to do my best to keep pace. Finally, he brings us upon a dead body laid against a shelter wall. A thick layer of sulfuric dust and debris covers the form.

He looks at me, goggles down. "Let's get some shopping done first, okay, man?" He kneels down, brushes off the body, and plumes of dust spill from the corpse. He goes for something near the dead woman's face, stands up, and hands me a thin gray linen scarf that's caked with dust and dirt. "Either we shop or another soulless will. Don't sweat it, man. That's yours now."

It doesn't feel great. A small ache pulls at my heart as I look down at the still body. Hard to tell her age, but not old by any means.

"Enough damage, and even an afterlife can end, man. See her head?" Cerutam yells near my ear now that the wind has picked up. He points from the woman's head to the wall. A patch of stone is embossed where dust clings rather than skips across. He grabs her hair and twists her head, showing the side that's been hidden from me, the side that's been caved in and ruined. "She either had something someone wanted or someone just felt like ending her for the fun of it. There's a lot of walkers like that in here, man."

It's despairing. Who was she and why would someone do this? What family did she have? Is this fate something she truly deserved?

Cerutam starts walking away, then stops, throws the back of his hand against my bicep, and chuckles a bit. "Or she ended herself by repeatedly ramming her own head against that shelter." He grabs my shoulder and leans in close. "It happens, man. The idea of a final end intrigues us all at times."

This sits with me, right next to the ache in my chest, next to the lies I've told this day, next to the longing for the boat, for clarity, for myself. *How long will it be before I find myself? Will I ever find myself—who I really am? Or will the intrigue of a final end find me first? My sanity succumbing to madness, lunacy prevailing over my once sound mind.*

My shoulders wear heavy on me, and my feet begin to drag. The linen scarf (I refuse to call it my own) clears the air and keeps labored breaths close, though my mouth still turns as dry as the cracked sulfurous ground. Over the course of our continued expedition, Cerutam shows me many things. All prove a previous assumption—that Tartarus isn't just a prison; it's damnation. I see walkers missing hands, missing limbs, some with gashes running across their faces sealed poorly by time, others with chunks taken from their thighs or arms. I see one missing their entire lower jaw, their scarf wrapped tightly around several times, creating a makeshift throat. Cerutam tells me these are all victims of the Maw.

"You run, you hide, you let your uneasy nerves gain footing while in the Maw's presence, and man, do you pay for it. The boatman has a job, and his lack of care for anything else is clear as day here in the circles of this prison. I myself was almost torn to bits on my entrance. When told to board the boat, I couldn't move. Neither my mind nor body wanted to go anywhere with that demon. Not really sure what came over me. Maybe it was mindless instinct, but something decided to force my legs to move and get on that boat before he lost patience with me just standing there stunned.

"Your *story*," Cerutam says, insinuating hesitant belief. "All of it is far-fetched and not something I suggest touting, ya hear? Anything too far out of the norm, anything that stands out around here, will gain attention, and attention isn't good. You need to blend in, man." His finger jabs hard into my chest this time. "You need a better story."

CHAPTER FIVE

Reprisal

"I've told you before, Cerutam, the boatman gave it to me, damn it. You took the same journey as I. What do you think? I killed the fucker, stole his dagger, then decided it was a good idea to walk my way voluntarily into this hellhole just so I could spend the rest of my days with your sorry ass?"

Cerutam just sits there, staring at the flame pit after breaking eye contact with me. He knows full well there is no conceivable way any human would have the capabilities to best a demon monster such as Karhon. Yet here we are, over an Earth year later, and from time to time, I am still getting badgered about these things—my dagger, my ring, my journey on the river. I wish he would just let the shit go. I've told him the truth (mostly). The only thing I've really hidden from him is the truth coins. So it would do us both well if he would finally believe what I'm telling him. Our stories really are quite different, and because of that, I don't hold it against him for questioning my tale. It's just become *fucking* annoying, and I don't wish to repeat or defend my own honesty any longer.

Cerutam and I get along pretty damn well compared to most other cell mates and groups, which I know we are both grateful for. And if it weren't for him, my earliest days here in the Lowest would have undoubtedly been much different. I owe him much. He didn't have to, but he kind of took me under his wing, showed me how to better my chances at avoiding trouble, showed me ways to survive in here. He explained how this godforsaken prison works, and in doing so, it became clear to me how much of an exception and outsider I am.

Every walker in Tartarus is considered soulless, myself included, but all others here came with their memories—and Tartarus coins, for that matter. Tartarus coins give the owner the option of a trial, where the warden and arbiters hear your reasoning for your wrongdoings, sins, and disrespect for your gift of life in the living world. Then you are judged based on your regrets and how you would have done things differently (if at all). All for the slight chance that the council of arbiters will deem you worthy and honest enough to spend the rest of your days in another region of the End Realm instead of Tartarus. This is astronomically rare, but still, many waste their coins on a trial with the council.

The other option with a Tartarus coin is to choose a specific circle (or region) of Tartarus to spend your eternity in. All the circles have their pros and cons, but they are all still prisons and are torturous hell in their own unique ways. The ability to choose your prison in exchange for your coin appeals to some. The only time this option is not available is when you have a Lowest coin, which means you have no say in the matter; you end up here—the lowest and worst of the Tartarus circles. Or like me, you have neither, which allegedly is unheard of.

Yeah, I feel real fucking special . . .

I have my two truth coins, but there is nothing I can use them for here in this circle it seems. I keep them hidden on me, taking the advice from Karhon to not trust anyone here and not lose such coins.

Lowest coins are reserved for the vilest of scum, the most twisted and immoral of beings that truly didn't deserve a life in the living world to begin with, in my opinion. And those are the life-forms I find myself surrounded by. I feel I simply don't belong here with them. On the other hand, I also often wonder—maybe I do. Even though I feel I would have been a decent and honest person while above and feel I would have had a great respect for my gift of life, I simply have no evidence of that. And I find this emotionally and spiritually crushing at times. It is why my main drive and desire currently is to find a way to reclaim my memories and to know the truth about my ring. If I have promised myself to another, I must get back to them. This is of the utmost importance to me.

Without another word, Cerutam gets up from the fire and proceeds to the corner he sleeps in.

I must get out. This circle, this prison—it's taxing me. The sick, demented, and mad minds within Tartarus only grow madder and more insane. My mind is still well enough that I am able to reflect—I'm still conscious and aware of the weight this place has piled on my mind, my sanity, in just this first year. *I must get out. Fuck, I hope this stupid plan works.*

I get up and make my way to my own corner, lying facing the stone wall, wishing once again we could do away with the blue flame and enjoy darkness while we slept. The flickering hue even reaches my hands, which rest in front of me, giving light to the reminder of the day I arrived on the shore. The vivid pain and sight of the soulless mark being seared on my left hand, marking me with where I'll belong forever—it all still echoes within me. Even the smell of my burning flesh has not been forgotten. The scar of the three intersecting swords is a constant reminder of many things: the last days I had with Karhon of the Rivers, my entrapment here in this lowest prison of Tartarus, my lost memory, and my longing to find answers. My mind narrows in on what is soon to come. In just two days' time, we have planned to attempt our escape, which in all honesty is absolutely fucking absurd of us.

Months back, a dareen (a walker species that resembles humans far more than they differ) named Tritang told us of a slip in the outer wall. One night he shared with us that a cell mate of his, roughly three hundred years in the past, attempted to get over the main wall of the Lowest. Even though the main wall appears to never end or to at least go on for an insurmountable height, Tritang "says" that his cell mate did make it to a section that had a short tunnel—a break in the solidified corpses where one could slither through and then descend their way down the outer side of the main wall. We aren't sure if we fully believe Tritang's tale, but it gives me a sense of hope, and my inner drive to find answers is so overbearing, so strong that even hearing a most likely completely fabricated tale of a crevice in the main wall is something that I have the inability to ignore and not investigate fully.

The dareen showed Cerutam and me exactly what section of the wall his cell mate had climbed, telling us that he was gone for several days before returning with the news that he had found such an escape passage. This portion of the claim gives us qualms for a few reasons. If he was gone for so long, then it is highly possible this passage through the stone will not simply be a straight ascent, but rather the cell mate could have gotten to a certain altitude and then traversed the wall in one direction or the other, therefore making it really difficult—if not impossible—for us to find the crevice just by starting our ascent where Tritang showed us.

There are so many variables here. How far up is the passage? What diameter is the passage? And again—did Tritang's cell mate stick to a mostly vertical climb, or did he end up traversing a different direction at some point? It is a really unintelligent endeavor to attempt to find this hole in the wall. The chances of us actually finding this needle in a haystack, even if it does actually exist, are stupidly low.

The other issue we have with this story is why Tritang's cell mate made the journey back down the inner side of the wall when he could have attempted to escape himself. When I posed this question, Tritang said his cell mate was too worried about getting caught on the outer side by the vast infantry patrolling it, knowing if he were caught that his soulless brand would be found on his hand and his capture would have resulted in a really brutal punishment—most likely ages spent in a solitude chamber or one of the under-dwelling areas known as the rack (or torture) dungeons.

Lastly, this prisoner was gone for several days. Was it even possible for a walker to climb that long of time without their body giving out and falling to their demise? Tritang had no further information regarding this, though Cerutam and I hope that since the main wall is not completely flat—the corpses in the wall make for some areas that stick farther out than others— we should be able to find ledges for us to rest our bodies and recuperate some before continuing the accent.

Furthermore, after three hundred years, did Tritang really remember the spot where his cell mate started his venture? Having the opportunity to speak with this prisoner would be a tremendous asset—if he were still walking this plane. Unfortunately, his existence was ended by a group of soulless that caught rumors of his knowledge of the wall. It's said the group of prisoners were not satisfied with his cooperation, or lack thereof, and Tritang ended up coming back to their shelter one evening to the sight of the man displayed in several pieces around the entrance. He may have been better off trying his luck against the infantry outside the main wall.

This quest is sure to result in the two of us failing miserably and ending up recaptured by Alastor's infantry. Still, we are dead set on this attempt. I believe Cerutam's reason for accompanying me on this climb is out of pure boredom—or in the hopes of finding his final end. He has been here in the Lowest for more than a thousand years, and though he won't admit to it, I figure he is trying his best to find his true end—to be caught and finalized to nothingness or to fall a monumental distance and find his end that way. I don't have a lot of faith or trust in Cerutam, but he also has never given me any specific reason not to. Overall, I just don't feel anyone here is worthy of much faith. The warning from Karhon to not trust anyone in Tartarus is something I heed and keep desperately close to heart—always.

Cerutam assures me, however, that his desire to escape with me is to aid in my goal of reaching the Fields of Asphodel. That is my plan and my true direction here. To get out of this hellhole and make my way there somehow. To eventually find the High Sanctum where I can then seek an audience with the arch-sorceress, Lunacrye, in the hopes of offering my truth coins in exchange for some answers: who I am; what this ring of mine really stands for; and what I want most of all, a full recovery of my memory. If full recovery is possible, I think I would do just about anything for that gain.

Ughhh! Can't fucking sleep. Way too much on my mind.

I get up briskly and step out of the entrance and into the sulfur haze. No destination in mind. This happens often when I can't lie still or keep a clear head—my mind just spirals. I know there is no winning over the spiral once it has started, so I get up and walk, mostly in anger, in frustration, sometimes for hours. *I can't take another year of this hell, much less a century or more like so many in here have.*

I could veer from the plan, start the climb of the wall tonight. I could even do so by myself, leave Cerutam at the cell and just head out on my own. I am eager to start. Asphodel is something I *need*. I must get out of this circle. I need to find who I am.

It is amazing to me how the hope I have to effectively escape and reach my goals has magically diminished all reason and logic when it comes to this plan. I know how insane it all is, and I know the chances of any success are practically null.

Yet the passion I have for reaching the truth is so impactfully strong that it tramples reason with undying resolve. I'm fully aware of the grandiose self-deception happening. Even still, being aware of it doesn't have any effect on taming the dream. Part of me actually believes this will work. This has to work. I have to escape, and I have to reach the High Sanctum.

I find myself close to the stone structure in which Tritang spends his days. He looks to be sitting at his flame pit. I walk up, peer in. Maybe it is worth seeing if I can possibly get any further missed information from the dareen. "Tang, mind if I join you?"

Tritang turns around. His big round brown eyes give me some unease. They are something I still find hard to get used to. Dareens have no eyelids, and their eyes are always one solid color, usually a brown or grayish blue. Their eyes look out of place to me; it's like looking at a puzzle that needs to be fixed.

"Nah, come on in, Nameless. Couldn't settle enough to sleep?" he poses as I sit next to him and begin staring into the empty flames.

"Pffft, what gave it away?"

"I could hear you coming. You rarely pass by at this hour without that leaden foot of yours. If you're out at this hour, patterns tell me it's because you're raging about something."

"I'm not going to disagree with you there. I'm restless as fuck tonight. Mind is racing a mile a minute, and you know I won't tell you when, but I am eager to try to find that passage in the main wall. I need to get out of here, Tang."

Tritang takes a deep breath, exhaling smooth and slowly, almost in a sigh. "I'm going to tell you something, Nameless." Tritang shuffles next to me, turning himself to face me a bit more than he was. "Is there a soulless in this prison that you think doesn't want out? We have all gone through the stage you're in, some of us a number of times over. You've been here for mere seconds compared to most, damn it. Figure out a way to get past it and be content with what you find around you. You will be here forever, just like every other forsaken corpse walking this land. You're not unique."

I give him silence in return, mostly because everything he said irritates me, making it easy for me to dig down even further into the pit of anger and frustration I am in tonight. I know I am a fresh prisoner here. I'm not blind to the fact that other soulless find this place just as crippling, depressing, and torturous as I. Having that thrown in my face by Tang wrenches at my bones though. If he thought I was raging before, I wonder what word he would choose to describe my physiological state now.

"I'm not fucking blind nor an idiot, Tritang," I say, stern. "I will get out of here though, some way, somehow, someday. I *am* going to find that same way through the wall your cell mate did, but I am not turning back around."

"Was all a joke, Nameless!" Tritang beams back as he throws his palms out to his sides. "Spouted falsity to give you some hope to hang on to until you could come to the conclusion on your own that you're damned and will be damned, here, forever. There is no fucking escape." He gets closer, and his breath crawls on my neck. I want to grab it and throw it off. My eyes close and tense; my teeth grate against each other. "There is no *fucking* passage in the wall, damn it!" he says.

Just as a scorpion has its reflex to sting, overcome with rage, hurt, and sorrow, I instantly find my hand around his neck with such force that I get us both up to standing. I feel my grip increase in increments as his windpipe collapses—crushed under my grip. Hearing the cracking of his trachea as I shove him hard into the stone wall behind propels me to sting even harder. His audible struggles continue while neck bones creak under my damning grasp. As I look deep in his lidless eyes, finding pain and fear, in which I revel, I unsheathe my dagger with my right hand and, in a single rapid motion, thrust the blade through the side of his skull behind his temple with such brutal intent that the hilt smashes against the left side of his face. All resistance stops, and I look over at the tip of my onyx blade protruding from the other side of his head. A gel-like ooze is spilling out, viscous, in no race to reach his jawline.

After screaming in his now lifeless face, I drag the weapon from the wound, still finding myself crushing his neck against the blood-spattered stone. I growl again in incendiary rage as I throw his soulless now ended corpse aside.

"FUCK!" I declare in a scream as I exit the encampment. With no desire to hide the dagger or my blood-ridden lower arm, I set out straight for the wall with even heavier leaden steps than those I came in with.

CHAPTER SIX

Ascent

S outheast is the direction in which Tritang showed us his cell mate had climbed (or not climbed at all apparently), and that is my bearing, eyes set hard on the vague hazy horizon. The enraged state I was in has resolved; however, I know the underlying anger—which is beyond rational—will linger for much longer, and so I feel content and at home in my fury and hatred. I'm content but driven and ready to get this ascent started right now, tonight—the near suicide mission of escaping this pit of the damned.

I catch myself from following my initial enraged intent of going alone. During the time in Tritang's encampment, I was not in control of complete rational thought. Now that I find myself thinking more clearly, I know I cannot make this journey without Cerutam. Not because he's needed, but because I told him this was something we would do together. He is under the impression that we are to leave to start our climb within days. Leaving him behind would be a dishonesty that—however convenient for me—I simply cannot allow myself to delve into. This is not a debate within me, though I do feel the pulling struggle of each option, like choosing which axe I want to be eviscerated with. Only in this case, one axe is morally unavoidable. If

49

I had people in the afterlife that I deemed true friends of mine, then my word to a petty criminal soulless like Cerutam I don't believe would matter in the least. I could, with no qualms, leave Cerutam behind and betray him with little to no internal issue. Unfortunately, Cerutam is as close to a friend as I have in the Lowest, and somehow, this makes it more binding to me, even if at the same time I feel this makes me a bit hypocritical and untrue to my true morality.

It does not matter to me if Tritang's tale is in fact false. Getting out of here is my direction, whether that ends with me in the Fields of Asphodel or with me in the hands of the infantry's guard. It does not matter—what matters is staying the course. Even though my time here in the Lowest has been limited, I know there is no way to my goals while within these walls.

Coming in at a bit of a run through our shelter's entrance is enough to wake Cerutam in the corner in which he rests. "Thought I heard you retire for the evening shortly after me," he says groggily, yawning.

"I tried, but like usual, I found myself unable to clear the busy mind taking residence in my head."

"Ah, one of those nights, huh, man?" His goggles move to his forehead. The sleep tries to cling while a sleeve clears it from his eyes.

"Yes, but not quite. We're leaving tonight, like . . . right now. Get your pack and let's go."

Cerutam shoots up a bit more, looking much more awake. "Wait, what? The plan was to wait until after the infantry has made their next march through so we know they won't be near again for days. That's still the safest plan, man."

"We both know that the infantry is not marching through tonight. That will still be in the days ahead. I'm not spending another night with this overwhelming my brain. The weight of this place grows heavier and *heavier* with each goddamned passing day. I can't wait. I'm starting the climb tonight," I declare as I thrust a finger toward the ground. "The choice to come is still your own. No hard feelings either way, and that's the truth."

Cerutam stands up, places his hands on his hips, and seems to give me a long contemplative stare. From the corner nearest me, I grab my pack, which holds several loose rocks, some shaped for cutting and other utility use, and some others that I gathered to tie onto our rope. We fashioned it from loose articles of clothing scavenged throughout the Lowest over the long months of our planning. I turn around after slinging the pack over my shoulder. Cerutam hasn't moved an inch, his statue working hard in a race to decision, his lenses overtaken by blue flames glaring into me and searching for understanding.

He gives a short toss of his hands outward and says, "Okay, let's go," in a sort of disapproving resignation.

Without delay, my travel out the doorway is closely met by a rushing Cerutam as he haphazardly manages to get his pack on his back. Not thirty yards into our directly eastern march, I lose Cerutam from my right side. I keep walking, but backward, as I've turned around to look his way. He quickly lets me know, "I've forgotten something. Don't wait up, man. I'll run right back!"

With that, he bolts back to the shelter. As I proceed with little care about his decision and no intention of slowing my brisk speed, confusion hits me a bit. *What the hell did he forget?* I laugh to myself as I think; other than our packs and the clothes on our bodies, the shelter contains absolutely nothing. Cerutam does in fact rush back quickly, with definite shortness in his breath and a somewhat tripped walk.

"What did you leave behind, ya dolt? Your monthly planner?"

"May sound dumb to you, Nameless, but that has been my . . . well, my home for the better part of two millennia. Had to say a goodbye."

Not offering any dissent, I nod with some understanding.

We are roughly a quarter day's journey from the eastern section of the wall we must reach, and only a few hours so far have been put between us and the shelter zone. It is a long trek, and I have been planning out when would be the best time (if at all) to divulge to Cerutam the fate of Tritang and his last words. It's something I find myself sorting out in a manipulative way. I fear if I tell Cerutam of all this before we put sufficient distance between us and the shelters that he could choose to bail on the venture and possibly seek out the infantry in retaliation, pointing them in my direct location. If I tell him too far into our journey, he could retaliate in other ways more directly, like shoving me off the heights of the wall or ending me in my sleep.

There is the option of not telling Cerutam of this at all, which seems the safest of the options cycling through my thoughts. I know well enough though that if I don't tell him, there is a really good chance this entire debate of options in my head will not be something I am able part ways with. The last thing I need while making this escape is for my mind to be plagued with this indecision and dishonesty. I need to be focused on the dangerous tasks at hand.

Our pace is steady and fast. The reddish tint that diffracts within the pale yellow air during the day hours in the Lowest starts appearing in gentle rolling waves, seen most clearly in areas of dense sulfur dust and other airborne particulates—a sign of the coming morning. *One more day cycle in the books for me and hopefully my last.* Using my judgment of when we left our shelter, along with the ruby tint becoming evident, I'm betting we're now within an hour of our destination.

It's a tricky object, this wall. From inside, the main wall goes unseen by us soulless until we are within a short distance of it, blocked by another wall of magical fog that has no color but acts almost mirrorlike. One can stand back from this fog and not know it's there at all. It seems to reflect its surroundings, giving the appearance of a never-ending sulfur plain of wastes, one you could walk forever, never reaching anything other than the continued view of endless horizon—a sure way to get most to turn back. Within a few feet of the fog, however, you can make out its deceit. The fog becomes a wispy white cloud that flows, twisting as though there are tiny creatures flying within its material.

"Hey, there's something you should know."

For the first time since departing, I stop in my tracks. Having been walking for so long, an unease pulses throughout my body like I have not stopped at all—that feeling you get when your body has grown so accustomed to monotonous movements that it still thinks it's in that repeating dance.

Turning, Cerutam breaks pace as well. "Mm, what's that?"

"Tritang is dead. I killed him last night after he tol—"

"Whoa, *what*? You crimed?" he interrupts. "And against the soulless who, if it hadn't been for them, we wouldn't even know of this way out?" He grabs me by the collar of my jacket. "This could easily bring the infantry through early if they hear of an ending crime. What the hell were you thinking, man?"

Cerutam's pissed. This is somewhat unexpected. I have never seen him get excited about crimes, even ending crimes, and it's not like he and Tritang were close by any means—at least not to my knowledge.

I shove him back, freeing my jacket. Sighing, I think to myself. *This already has me frustrated.* "Ack, just get the hell off me, firstly. I was walking past his encampment last night, and he didn't mind me stopping in. I mentioned I couldn't sleep, as I was busy in my head about escaping via the passage—"

"Ah, yes, hospitality is obviously reason to end someone!" Cerutam mocks, which results in his receipt of a gaze he has gotten from me before, the one where I am interrupted, a disrespect I have particular disdain for.

"Let me finish, damn it. There's more to it than that. He told me this was all a hoax. He got in my damn face and tried to make me feel like a fool for believing such drivel, that it was a story made up to give me some hope and get me through the initial struggle of being imprisoned here. I lost it, Cerutam. I didn't want to believe it. I felt abused, mocked, and hurt. How dare he lie to me about something like that or to at least not inform me of his deceit sooner? I threw his corpse aside and beelined right for the wall, knowing I had to still try, even if it meant concluding that Tritang did lie to us. I caught myself though. I couldn't leave you at the shelter without at least a parting word, so I veered course to make that stop first."

Cerutam's pacing side to side with his hands on his hips again, taking turns looking down at the ground of cracked stone and off in the distance in contemplation. "So you were told of this, and still you decided to allow me to follow you all this way without saying a word of it, tricking me into a position where I am now close enough to the wall to feel the allure of escape and the curiosity of Tritang's tale still possibly having merit? You've made my decision on the matter more of a predicament than it would have been if you had been honest and clear with me sooner. For example, before we even stepped foot out of our own shelter! Damn it, man. You've lost some of my trust, Nameless." He stops, looks up at me. "This will not be forgotten."

"Turn around now. That's still an option for you," I say while pointing west toward the shelter region. "I withheld what I felt I needed to until I felt safe sharing it, Cerutam. This is the Lowest. We are not amongst righteous souls here. Everyone watches their back as if there is nothing but betrayers in this land, and we all have good reason for it. I would be pissed if I were in your position too, but make your decision and make it now, because I am moving forward."

"You mean to find a passage in the wall that you were just told is not there by the same dareen who told us of its supposed existence in the first place? I mean . . ." He chuckles. "Come on, man."

Cerutam's being snide and rightfully so. What he's hearing from me is asinine. Only a fool would still chase after such an endeavor after hearing of it being pure fabrication.

"You know my story and of my ambition. I cannot stay here. I have one goal, and as I see it, there's only one way of getting closer to that goal, and that is getting the fuck out of Tartarus. I either attempt escape via the wall at a different location or I try ahead, where Tritang showed us. This way, at least I'll feel like I am also finding the truth of this all."

Cerutam stops his side-to-side movements, and for some time stands still, hands on hips and face to the noxious yellows of the stone on which we so familiarly endure. He slowly brings his goggles down to ease his stare on the cracked sulfur, the look of puzzlement and quandary easily seen across his stature. *Fuck, I don't have time for this. This is wasting time. Either come with or turn back, man, but ya gotta figure it the fuck out right now.*

I walk forward, placing a hand on his shoulder. "No hard feelings either way, Cerutam. I value the time you've contributed to working together on this, and the times you've had my back down here are both countless and remembered. I mean it."

With his eyes still drawn to the stone, I take my leave. After a handful of paces, I can hear his decision: footfalls crumbling the sulfurous wastes behind me, though they never fully catch up to be at my side. Internally, I shrug it all off. It may be cold of me, but I really don't care either way about his destination at this point.

⊛ ⊛

"Chronos, what has you troubled at this time?"

Michael had seen this look of puzzled concentration on Chronos many times before. Being the most potent time warlock in the realm had many afflictions amongst its blessings.

"I felt the chime of two coins ring upon ground cycles ago. Something about its happening has been unclear and distant to me. Any *time* I cannot fully resolve becomes a plaguing calculation to which all my energy gravitates. You know this," Chronos replied.

"The last *time* that plagued you this way, I recall it being a significant consumption of power . . . as well as a significant burden to properly solve."

"Your computation is accurate." Chronos slouched down even farther with a hand over his faceted insect eyes and forehead, showing his distress.

Michael knelt down next to Chronos, gracefully folding an angelic wing around the raised dais on which the time warlock sat. "What do you need, brethren?"

"Time, my friend. I must give it time."

✪ ✪

Getting to the wall and beginning the climb escapes my mind. My thoughts are replaced with the incident back at the shelter zone. I still feel no remorse for what transpired, rationalizing it with the fact that I was betrayed and lied to. Even if him telling me that it was all a hoax was the lie, in my mind, it was still an act of betrayal. Then there's the account of Tritang's attitude toward me. Getting in my face about it was uncalled for, was it not? Then again, was it not uncalled for to drive a dagger through his skull? Although I don't have any regrets, it hits me now that I did not need to kill him. I could have easily just walked out of his encampment, not even voicing my anger to him, and been on my way—could've walked off the escalated emotions I was dealing with during that time.

Taking a look at the information from a reporter's point of view opens up several new avenues of thinking for me.

The man who killed the dareen did so in a fit of rage. He was not fully in control of his emotions or actions. He had not contemplated the actions prior to committing to them and therefore did not take the time to think about his options and make a conscious and rational decision. In hindsight, he concluded that he did what he felt he had to. He felt betrayed. His goal and purpose were to regain lost memories so he can know who he is, where he came from, and if he has a partner whom he is vowed to. In his mind, anything that got in the way of that purpose was a threat, and he would seemingly do anything to get closer to the end of his endeavor.

This all speaks volumes to me, bringing up a question I haven't spent time on for a long while. What if I truly am meant to be soulless down here in the End Realm? The recent fit of rage resulting in a brutal account of murder is evidence enough that I quite possibly could have committed such acts of violence while above in the living world. Truth still is, I know nothing of the man I was while above. Was he any different than me now? Would he have taken the same action at Tritang's encampment? *How stupid will I feel—will I be able to forgive myself if I do end up succeeding in finding what I have lost, only to then know I deserve the designation the End Realm gave me?*

Even though I'm aware that I lost my shit and ended someone's afterlife, I still feel confident that I was once a good man. A good person that took the gift of life seriously and would not so easily lose emotional and physical control to the degree of ending another's gift of life. But . . . who knows? *I need to find my past so I can—*

"Okay, okay, slow down a bit now," Cerutam interrupts my reflection. "Let's do this part together, yeah, man?"

Looking up, I instinctively take a step back, for I've almost walked right into the fog wall without realizing it. Close enough now that the twirling sweeping fog is within touching distance, I lift my arm and arc my hand through without haste.

"Here we are," Cerutam notes as he closes the gap and is now standing next to me at my right side—first time since making the decision to continue.

I sweep my hand back through, now in a reverse manner. For a moment, I just stare into the magic of the misty wall, nostalgia rampantly invading me, bringing me back to the starry liquid of the river that brought me here. *Oh, how I wish to be on that boat again with Karhon.*

"Ready?" I ask Cerutam with a nod.

"There won't be any turning back . . ." Cerutam states as if he is reminding himself of our deal to not give up. Under no circumstances are we to head back to the shelter zone once we pass the fog; we swore. We're to climb and search for an exit until we succeed or die trying. "Yeah. Yeah, I'm ready, man," he says, psyching himself up. "Let's go."

Without hesitation, I look from him to the fog and walk straight through. Passing through is uneventful, just like last time when the dareen showed us the location. The fog's magic is reflective—yes, twisting and twirling—and its waves do seem to react with the motion of passing objects, but past that, it is nonexistent. You can't feel it in any way.

Cerutam passes through alongside me, the macabre wall of corpses only about twenty yards ahead of us. I look up and pan left to right. I am quickly able to find the important area of large skulls we are looking for.

Pointing their way, I say, "There's our patch of imp skulls."

He throws his goggles over his eyes. "Damn, that's some luck, man! When Tritang brought us here, it took us hours of searching to find the spot."

"I want this more than fucking anything, Cerutam." I look over his way. "I made a point to memorize the route far more accurately than Tang ever had."

Wanting to start the climb right away, I start my pace over to the patch of skulls. There are imp corpses throughout the entirety of the wall, but this specific spot has a high concentration of them within a twenty-foot or so radius and is roughly four stories up the wall. The concentration of them doesn't hold any particular significance that we know of other than this being where Tritang's cell mate told him he had started his ascent.

"Should we rest first?" Cerutam asks. "It was not a short travel to get us here, man. What's the rush?"

"Come on, you know what my damn rush is," I say with a toss of my head. "Plus, you were worried that the end crime of Tang would bring in the infantry sooner. So then, let's just get our asses moving." I grab hold of the nearest imp skull just a foot or so above my head.

"All right, man. I'm with ya. Not like we would be able to get any sleep around here anyway, I'm sure."

As I look down for a bone or body part to use as my second foothold, the imp skull that my right hand's firmly grasping breaks free a bit from the wall. Not only does my hand slip off, but I, too, have to take the short hop off the wall back to the ground so as to not altogether fall flat on my back.

"Damn, I thought the wall was way more solid than th—"

Before I can finish my remark to Cerutam, my train of thought halts, attention seized by the imp skull that cracked loose. It's not only loose. It's coming out of the fucking wall in full form.

Cerutam and I backpedal a few hurried paces.

"What the *fuck* is that? The damn imp is alive!" I exclaim.

The sand-colored rusty red imp corpse is now all the way out of the wall, posing low and defensive on the ground, snarling with chattering fang-filled jaws and ready to pounce at anything that comes within distance.

"Why is this happening?" Cerutam questions as he sweats and quakes. "We were here with Tritang and touched the wall several times. I—I don't understand."

As Cerutam finishes, dozens more imp corpses begin shifting within the wall. Sheets and patches of rock crash to the ground, falling from areas between the shifting corpses. Within seconds, amongst the fallen plasterwork debris, there are too many imps to even count, all posing threateningly on the ground in front of us, snarling and inching closer.

"We run. We turn and run, man," Cerutam says, grabbing my shoulder, pulling on me in fear. "There's no other way out of this."

He turns round, starting his mad dash. I turn to grab and hold him back but become solidified after my first firm step, stunned at what I see between us and the fog wall. We are now trapped, trapped between the deadly snarling imps. And them—in front of the fog—Alastor of Chains, his herald, and his five officers.

CHAPTER SEVEN

Woe

"This is where they rang."
Chronos was down on his knee, touching the solid stone ground with his hand, which was dressed in his emerald exoskeleton. Seeing that he was deep in concentration as he kneaded at the stone, Michael took the opportunity to view their surroundings, enjoying the awful and inspiring view of the Deliverance Gates. The entrance to this existence, the sealed door and immense wall, had never bored the angel.

"Truth coins . . ."

It took a second or two, but this snapped Michael out of his reverie.

"Serious?" Michael stooped down beside the warlock. "When was the last time we saw that currency manifest here?"

"It was just over three hundred years ago. Still . . . their occurrence is rare, and I am not certain why two would be given, but two were dropped upon this ground and retrieved by their owner. I can see now—these are carried by someone clouded to me. I cannot see their past or present clearly."

Michael could see the struggle Chronos was in. When there was a time rift (when Chronos could not accurately see the past

61

or present), it was a sort of agony to him. His entire purpose was to know the past and to keep record of the universe, so when there was a hole in time, the job of calculating and finding the truth consumed him.

They both darted their eyes up as they heard a woman's shrieking pleas in the near distance ahead. Her heavy panting, terrified echoes, and the sound of branches being haphazardly snagged and broken proliferated as she came into their view. She broke out of the brush area just ahead and, nearly tripping over herself, hung her head low as she braced herself with hands on her knees. The woman's arched back only got the chance to heave twice with heavy exacerbated breathes before a racing black wispy cloud darted with surreal speed in front of her, stooping low in a crouch to the stone. As she was taking a step back and beginning another assailing scream, the black cloud lunged forward, atomizing midair into a grim cloaked figure. She became besieged by the assailant and, after a loud thunderous sound as if a heavy door were slammed shut midair, was immediately crushed to the ground.

Silence fell. The cloaked one stayed low on their knees, rocking slowly back and forth while facing away from and blocking any view the two nearby would've had of the woman.

"Is that . . .?" whispered Michael.

"Yes, the Maw," Chronos replied with the added involuntary clicking of his mantis-like mandibles.

"I've never met him. From what I know, I do not envy his appointment."

"If our Devil-God was asked of his favorite, he would in fact choose." Nodding forward, Chronos continued, "And he would choose Karhon of the Rivers without needing to even think on it. He was Hades's closest confidant." Chronos clicked.

They both remained motionless. Michael was waiting for the boatman to move from his current state and position.

"What is he doing?" Michael asked softly, still in whisper. "Why is he swaying so?"

"Archangel, he is sobbing. Though without tears."

Michael looked from Chronos back to the Maw as the time warlock continued. "See . . . yes, our Devil-God Hades did take his eyes. Took from him the ability to cry and to see the atrocities he must carry out. Though that was purely of compassion, unfortunately Karhon's murderous reality is still oppressively harsh on his soul. He suffers much trauma."

Chronos slowly got up and with a hand on Michael's arm ushered him as well. The cloaked one stayed in his position while the two made their way to him. As they made their closing steps, Michael saw over the boatman's shoulder the body of the woman. Aghast, he unconsciously brought a hand over his mouth, clearly seeing the damage displayed on the smooth patch of stone now in front of them. From just under the woman's left shoulder down to her hip bone was completely gone, leaving a bloody void where her breast, heart, and lung once were. The Maw's single massive bite had left rough jagged cuts straight through her sternum and rib cage, leaving the back half of her rib bones still there protruding out from what was left of the meaty mess.

Nothing audible came from the boatman, his hooded figure still looking down, rocking slowly back and forth.

Chronos sat down cross-legged right next to the ghastly reaper. "It has been some time, old friend," the warlock clicked, but even after a sound pause, he received no reply. He placed his hand on the shrouded cloaked thigh of their company. The warlock could see inside him, past and present, and could see and feel his current grief. "Tonight . . . I can see tonight has been a difficult one, Karhon."

The boatman gradually stopped his somber forward and backward sway. "Ten so far," he replied lowly in his graveled voice. "I beg of them to not, yet they run."

From where he stood just behind the two, Michael could hear their conversation, as well as Chronos's clicking within pauses. He hadn't known Chronos knew Karhon so well, but it seemed as though they were close in relationship or had a past that Michael did not previously know of. As he'd mentioned before to Chronos, he did not envy the boatman's position and responsibilities to the realm, and now, after witnessing firsthand the brutally vicious action taken and the trauma Karhon was tormented with, he felt so even more. At the same time, he now had a newfound respect and admiration for the Maw. He had heard so many stories about the Maw that were twisted in a way, making the boatman to be easily seen as an evil entity whose sole desire was to feed on poor frightened souls only wanting to reach their final destination.

"I have come here to help calculate the past. There is a rift in time that I must resolve and catalog. I think you could aid me, my dear old friend."

"Do what I can, Father," was Karhon's dismal-sounding reply whilst not budging from his depressing pose.

"There is something I cannot see."

For the first time, Karhon looked up in the direction of Chronos's voice, and after a minor tilt of his head, he offered a loud "Ha!" and with his massive ominous smile, ended with, "So alike thee and I."

Michael could only venture the sudden humor was undoubtedly in reference to the Maw's stonelike blindfold and Chronos currently being unable to see the history of these two truth coins and their owner. The demeanor of the interaction between the two seemed to change drastically with that almost sarcastic expression and humor the boatman offered the timekeeper. Both now were in a more alert posture, and the air had a sense of opportunity and maybe even excitement, as if the mangled woman that lay there with her lifeless eyes left open had altogether disappeared.

"Have you seen truth coins pass through here recently? I can see two falling to the stone just over there, but—"

"Aye! A man possessing two came through the gates. Here, I will show thee!" The boatman, with his constant sinister-looking smile, excitedly brought his sharply armored hand to the face of Chronos. The paw of Karhon was huge, and the warlock's insect-like skull became only visible to Michael through the gaps between the boatman's long armored fingers.

Michael was familiar with this act and the magic the time-keeper was endowed with. Obviously so was Karhon. Chronos had the ability to contact anything, living or not, and to see of its past. Karhon, placing his hand on Chronos, offered the warlock the opportunity to see all of the boatman's past and current happenings, as well as even his feelings. No doubt that Chronos already knew all of not only Karhon's past, but everyone's past here in the End Realm without needing physical contact. The issue here was the rift in time he was needing to fill with facts. When there was a rift, the information of memories could only be transferred if the owner of the memories gave the data of their own free will. Being that the boatman had firsthand memories and experiences with the objects relating to this particular rift, he was a great vessel to gain such otherwise invisible facts from and to help fill the hole in time that Chronos had to fully calculate and record.

Transfer of the data took only as long as it took Karhon to cycle through it in his mind however he chose. He could think on and relive every image and word spoken if he liked, and all would then be seen by Chronos in the same manner, or he could cycle through it quickly and only show select information to Chronos that he felt most useful. This all gave the vessel of the memories the ability to hide things as well; however, that took an exceptional amount of will power, for anything the vessel thought of or reimagined is what Chronos would then see in real time.

Twisting darkness and lighter tones spiraled round, merging into a more real scene of a walk up to a man with a slight topside view, as if seen from a taller perspective. The view was faded shapes of only contrasts; almost no detail was seen. Only adolescent and the most basic of vision was available, like seeing only in silhouettes.

"What name does thou bare?" The view tilted on its axis to the left.

"I do not know my name . . . nor anything of my past, really," came forth from the lightened silhouette in front of a densely darkened background containing almost no discernible shapes at all. Only subtle soft tones of dark contrast were seen flowing behind the shape of the man.

Internal thoughts that this man did not belong here echoed and bounced within.

"What coin have you?"

"These are my only pos—"

The tilting view dove down with weight and speed and magnified exponentially as the vision twisted round and round again, diving into the two coins held out in the outline of a human palm. After reaching the hand of coins, everything became black again with the same initial twisting darkness and lighter tones of before, spiraling and weaving in and out of visions and outlines of a boat's front mast, the shoreline of a river, and the first-person perspective of handing a silhouette of a man a short-bladed weapon. Amongst this weaving in and out of imagery, the resounding echoes of a rocky harsh voice repeated over and over.

"My soulless one . . ."

"Tartarus . . ."

"Tartarus . . ."

"Not supposed be here . . ."

"I shall deliver thou . . ."

The voices came and went in different orders, at times over-lapping each other, making them difficult to interpret. Then the circular motion of the twisting contrasts became sporadic in direction, becoming governed by no specific pattern at all. The imagery spiked into a mess of fast motions and directions. Chaos.

The chaotic shifting views soon were joined by spontaneous internal mental pleas.

"Do not run this one . . ."

"I plea, do not flee, for I—"

"Do not chase her . . ."

"The woman. She just a young woman. I not want to harm . . ."

"Do not . . ."

"Do not."

Emotion and feelings of turmoil and depression beyond explanation took root and consumed the thought processes and state of the minds. Michael could tell something was amiss. The timekeeper and the boatman were both struggling as if Karhon's gauntlet were welded to the face of Chronos. His insect-like hands were now each on Karhon's forearm in an unsuccessful attempt to push away and sever the union.

Seeing the distress the two were bound in, Michael inter-vened. Taking hold of the boatman's hand that was clenched to Chronos's skull and pushing off firmly with a boot on the warlock's shoulder gave the angel enough leverage to break the two free of each other. The three of them having to recuperate from the stumble and imbalance gave enough time for the diz-ziness Chronos had succumbed to to wear off.

"You okay, brethren?"

Shaking his head a bit and clicking audibly, Chronos responded, "Yes . . . Yes, I am fine, Michael. Thank you for aiding us." Chronos looked to Karhon then. "We both found ourselves caught in a fairly afflictive situation at the end there."

A hand of exoskeleton and hemolymph was placed on Karhon's shoulder. The boatman offered a somber sounding,

"Mm-hmm." With his visor again pointed down at the woman's corpse, his demeanor looked to have sunken back to sullenness.

The time warlock stood up, turning to his guardian.

"What my dear friend here has just allowed me to see is troubling. The two truth coins . . ." Chronos paused for a moment while bringing a hand up to the right side of his head, turning his thumb and next two fingers outward in a show of disbelief and wonder. "Belong to a soulless."

"That's—wait." Michael furrowed his brow. "That's unheard of. Soulless arrive with manifested Tartarus coins or sometimes coins of the Lowest. Nothing more or less, ever. Truth coins are far too much a gift to be given to a soulless."

"Indeed." Chronos nodded. "Michael, there are no other unsolved calculations in *time*. This is the only rift currently, and I can tell you with absolute certainty that there has never been any account of a truth coin bestowed upon a soulless." Chronos took hold of Michael's arm again as he took a few strides back toward where the coins had contacted the dense ground. "Something is wrong here." The warlock looked up to meet the angel's solid white eyes. "We must go."

He turned back to Karhon, who still knelt in sorrow. Leaving Michael ahead, he strode back to the boatman and knelt down behind him slightly off to Karhon's left side, resting his hand as he previously had on his shoulder. "The next hour is a new hour, as tomorrow is another day. Give it time, my dear friend, do not run from your sorrows. Embrace them." Chronos then stood up. Before turning back to Michael, he wished Karhon fair well. "May your burdens of tomorrow be much less than today's."

Back at his guardian's side, he began the short walk back to the gates.

"Chronos, he called you Father. Is he your—?"

"There was a time, archangel." Chronos sighed. "Now I consider him a very dear friend."

No more eye contact was made between the two. In fact, Michael had now noticed the warlock's head hanging to the stone at his feet much like Karhon's had been moments ago. Reaching their previous location, Chronos fell down to place an open hand once more on the dark slate upon which the two truth coins had once rang.

"We must go. Now," demanded Chronos.

And with that, the archangel braced his time warlock by the shoulders, and with just a few beats of his massive ethereal wings, the two were at such heights one would not be able to see them from the stone on which they had stood mere seconds ago.

CHAPTER EIGHT

Chamber

Cerutam continues to dash toward the warden and his company. Quite possibly, that actually is the safer of the two directions. I have never heard of the imps coming alive, nor are they one of the species amongst us walking the End Realm (to my knowledge at least), so what the imps are capable of, as well as their intention, is a mystery to me. However, between their audible snarls and their threatening poses I'm confident they would attempt to kill me if I were to engage in the pursuit of ascending the wall.

As Cerutam gets within paces of Alastor, he slows, and Alastor begins drawing a spell in the air. The spell looks to be directed my way. I raise my hands in a sign of surrender. I really have no other choice in the present situation. Though I would do anything to continue escaping, I know that any attempt to flee the warden and his officers would surely result in an abruptly quick end to me. They are inescapable from this distance. Alastor finishes tracing his spell and activates it with a push of his palm. The orange glow of the tracing rushes forward.

Ahhh, fu—ck.

The spell is like a falcon riding an air current. I tuck myself in as much as I can. My eyebrows and cheeks reach for each other, preparing for the spell to smash into its target. But it races right past my side. A hefty breath leaves me. *Holy shi—! He missed?* I look back to Alastor. He's not readying another spell. *What the hell. Was it not for me?* I turn and follow it again with a swivel of my head. The glow disperses and separates midair into arcing streams as it reaches the army of imps at the base of the wall. The imp corpses leave the ground in magical levitation and begin contorting violently in the air as they float back to different heights of their home, each one of them moving their bodies in snapping unnatural ways as they begin molding back into the vast wall, becoming lifelessly glued into solid forms once again—their return to their fate, their fate of timeless art.

Alastor barks out, "Stay put, soulless!"

They begin advancing on my position. Cerutam is taken at the arm by Alastor, his herald and officers following close behind in the typical V formation they are always seen in. I stay put, but something seems amiss with Cerutam as they get close. The excited worry and fear he exhibited in his mad dash from the imps looks to have vanished. He seems surprisingly content.

"You are found guilty of attempting escape and will be taken in as such," barks the warden as he stops his advance, having reached me. "Rahkni!" Alastor commands, looking over to his highest-ranking officer.

Rahkni comes straight at me, the dark angel I've met once before feathered in dense gray down across his muscular build, his jet-black wings shining with iridescence through the hellish ruby tint of the dusty sulfuric air. Some say that Rahkni is even more intimidating than the warden himself—a declaration I won't be found arguing against. My arms are forced behind my back, held with inescapable strength.

I lie, "We were exploring the outer reaches and—"

"Do not attempt to mislead me, soulless," Alastor interrupts, then looks down to Cerutam, who is still held captive at the bicep. "Your cell mate here has told us of your intention, so spare us your deceit."

As I glare at Cerutam, he curls his mouth in a sadistic smirk. "What? Why?" I ask in disbelief.

Letting a short chuckle out, Cerutam replies, "Ah, I knew I could use your weakness as a means to get another trial. I alerted them of the plan several months ago and of our exact date as soon as it was settled on." Cerutam continues on, now with a sense of irritation: "With your damn impatience after ending Tang, I had to think quickly, so after we left the shelter, I ran back in and wrote a message on the wall for the warden, figuring he would be coming soon to investigate the end crime."

"I can't fucking believe you." It takes all my willpower and more to stop myself from attempting a charge at Cerutam. "I trusted you, damn it! And you sold me out for a fucking trial? You know you don't have a chance in hell at persuading the council!"

"Eh." Cerutam shrugs. "I'll take the extra chance with the council over following you around in your foolishly blind pursuits, damn idiot."

"Fuck you, man! I should have ended you as I did Tang," I say to him with a low sharp register accompanied by a damning glare. I'm more firmly held back by Rahkni now, overwhelmed with such anger that I haven't noticed how much I've been fighting against the dark angel's shackled grip.

Alastor takes a stern and heavy step forward. "Enough of this." He huffs, then points my way. "Take him to the pierce chamber," he orders Rahkni, then turns on a heel back to face Cerutam.

"Wait! No, please!" I lunge forward as best I can, begging in exasperation. "I need to get to Asphodel! I need to speak with the arch-sorceress, Lunac—"

Alastor spins around and barks inches away from my face—so close the dust in the air blasts sharp against me, his breath a raging oven, melting me back against Rahkni. "How dare you speak my sister's name!" The warden straightens up, squaring his shoulders, towering in dominion. "A soulless does not have the honor to mention the name of such authority and grace."

Sister? What the fuck?

"I need answers, sir. I need to find my past and my memories. That is my reason for attempting escape. Karhon said only two can offer truths about my past, and she is one." I say it as fast I can in fear of being cut off. I take a moment to catch my breath. The warden stares down on me but seems to give me minor space to speak. "I have two truth coins, Alastor. Please, I will do anything to get to the arch-sorceress."

Alastor's stare into me is blink-less. He turns his back on me and the dark angel clenching my hands in a knot at my back. "To the pierce chamber with him," he shouts over his shoulder to Rahkni. "The other is a dishonorable cowardly rat and will suffer the worser fate—*the pit.*"

Hearing this, Cerutam steps back quickly with a look of shock and worry worn on his face. "No . . ." He shakes his head. "You said—you said I would get a second trial for aiding you."

"I have no reason to keep my word to a dirty soulless like yourself. You damned yourself further by making the immoral choice of betraying someone who thought you a friend," Alastor says, his bark calm but finalizing.

At this, Cerutam says, "No, you won't take me to the pit." He turns and begins running—to the fog wall.

The warden conjures his whip with a hasty spell tracing. It appears instantly within his right hand. The metal slatted sections of the heavy whip made up of links of chromed metal hit the cracked sulfurous floor with enough force that a large plume of the acrid dust explodes off the ground, clouding my legs and those close enough.

Within seconds, Alastor launches the whip straight at Cerutam. The hit cracks right above Cerutam's knee. The chromed metal links are enough to effortlessly tear through him. The severed part of his leg falls to the ground, as does he in a haphazard tripped manner. His hands fly out in attempt to balance himself, but he falls hard, crashing to the stone ground. He screams out in agony as he struggles to keep himself up on his one good knee while bracing the rest of his weight with a hand on the ground. The attempt to drag himself to the fog wall away from the warden proves difficult as the lower half of his oozing red leg lies severed a meter behind him. The act looks pathetic and feeble, as he is still screaming in pain while gaining little ground as he drags his body across the dust-covered rock. I actually feel pity for him; there simply is no chance of escaping Alastor's ruling judgment.

Alastor lashes out again. This time, the whip hits Cerutam so hard in the center of the back that he's lifted airborne, with his arms spread out wide from the force. The force is so strong that his back arches like an archaic bridge, destined to fall and crumble. The kinetic energy shoved through Cerutam's torso is so immense his chest explodes outward in a crimson mist of blood. The blood, along with pieces of flesh and bone, rains to the ground, but not the rest of Cerutam's mutilated body. He stays suspended in the air due to a quickly produced hex the warden somehow managed to complete in the short time between the whip smashing against his back and his body being pushed airborne.

The warden, using his other hand, stretches out toward Cerutam's barely recognizable now silent corpse. He brings his outstretched fingers into a clenched fist, which makes Cerutam's corpse jerk suddenly. Alastor has a magical hold of what's left of the traitor. Turning at the waist slowly, he points himself and his fist to the main wall. Cerutam's body follows the magical order and hold the warden has on it. His corpse contorts in sharp unnatural motions just as the imps did when being moved, and the body of Cerutam gradually shifts to the color of rusty sand, matching that of the wall as he is pressed unwillingly into the structure. His body becomes breathless stone then. His face . . .

it haunts—wide eyes and an open mouth in a screaming and painful expression is all that's left to be seen of the cell mate Cerutam, who I once knew.

He shrugs. "The wall for you, then . . ." comes low from under his breath. "Let's move," Alastor commands with volume as the metal slatted whip he wields fades from existence like a ghost. His outstretched hand that controlled the fate of Cerutam's body now relaxes at his side.

Rahkni asks, "How long in the chamber, lord?"

"It is not your concern. I will retrieve him myself."

With this, Alastor traces a repeating circular spell in the air while vocalizing in a bestial language with sharp enunciations. A portal that shows as an oval window of frosted weaving glass as tall as the dark angel is conjured beside the two of us.

"I'm done here. Take him," Alastor says with a heavily tossed hand.

Rahkni walks me the few steps to the portal and shoves me with such force my feet leave the surface below, and in I travel, headfirst.

There is no travel time whatsoever. I land hard on the ground as if my momentum from being shoved has landed me on the same rocky land from which my feet just left. But I know the portal succeeded in taking me elsewhere—my nose, throat, and lungs stop burning from the caustic sulfur. The relief almost causes me to choke. Never thought clean air could feel so awkward. I blink a few times more just to make sure my eyes are actually open. I see nothing. It's pitch-black. No light lives here. The ground is smooth, smoother than that of the land near the wall where I just was, and feels much cooler to the touch. Nothing feels coated in yellow dust or rock particulates either. The floor makes me think of clean washed stone that's been cooled by the night sky and is waiting patiently for the warmth of a rising sun.

This is going to take some balance. With no visual to give myself bearing, a faint dizziness wraps me in its hold. I do my best and get myself up from the ground. The cool stone greets my feet—a sensation and a temperature they all but forgot existed. The chill the cold stone gifted my face starts wearing thin. I can feel the pain setting in now from the right side of my head and ear being smashed against the ground with my full weight behind the impact. I reach up with a hand and put pressure on the side of my head. "Ugh, fuck that hurts."

I almost jump at my own voice, not expecting it to sound so loud. It really makes me take note of the still air and deep silence. The side of my head above and around my ear is wet and warm—blood. My hand slides as I increase pressure on the wound, trying to extinguish some of the flames.

I assume Rahkni hasn't followed me through, else I'm sure he would already have me restrained again.

Alone.

I walk slow and carefully, my other hand held out in front, hoping to prevent myself from colliding into what may lie ahead. *One . . . two . . . three . . .* My hand reaches a wall, cool smooth stone, feeling the same as the floor. Pacing the wall left does not get me much farther; I'm met with another wall with the same characteristics. My head wounds ache harshly, waves crashing against a cliffside, eroding the cliff's stubbornness and desire to stand tall. I let my hand slide down the wall while I fall in the corner to a sitting position with my knees bent and out to one side. I let my hand go all the way to the floor, and the rest of my weight I surrender to be caught by the wall. I'm huddled in the corner. Or maybe the corner is holding me.

I have no idea where the portal has taken me and no knowledge of the pierce chamber the warden spoke of, though this isn't what I expected. As I lie against the cold stone corner, physical exhaustion sets like drying concrete, now being the first time I've let my body rest for . . . my memory escapes me. My brain's fogged. I cannot even muster the energy to recall how long it has been since the restless night on which I ended Tritang and set course for the main wall. Mental exhaustion from all that's transpired, from being betrayed by Cerutam to his final end and ill fate of becoming part of the wall, to my plan of finding the passage out of Tartarus being stopped dead in its tracks and my current predicament, where light does not exist and an even more rooted feeling of aloneness has burrowed itself into my chest cavity, bringing on a seemingly endless emptiness that I so long to have filled. The culmination of the past day and lack of sleep finally bears down on me.

A thought fills my head now, the first of its kind. I should have run as soon as I saw the tall standing demonic equine figure at the foot of the fog. I want what Cerutam and Tritang have now. I want this all to end. There is no getting out of this prison, this cage of despair and hollowness. Even Karhon told me there was no escape. *Why do I hold on to this unrealistic hope for answers and a future made of my own will and fate? Where did this drive originate? Where was the beginning of such endeavor and hope? Where did the hell-bent pursuit of—hmm . . .*

I do not move my head or redirect my line of sight, still blindly staring at the nothingness, the black void that steals the power from my eyes, but my mind goes to my left hand, which still lies there, palm up on the chill bleak floor. Unmoved since it fell there during my surrender to this corner is not only my hand, but the river's gift to me. My ring. Though I cannot see it, my mind and energy go to the heavy deep bronze jewelry. My ring . . .

A pool slowly wells, and without the aid of a blink, wets its own slow warm river down the valley of my face, hugging the baseline of my nose till it disperses into the fault line of my lips.

It was this ring. This gift of promises. This gift of devout commitment. This gift of shared life. This was the source of power that has propelled me on the direction and journey I find myself on—the real reason I am so driven to find answers and gain possession of the memories lost during my extraction from the world above. Something is telling me (even though I played through this in my mind several times prior and came to the conclusion that I didn't yet know for certain if this was a ring of wedlock or not) that this truly is the case—it is a ring of wedlock, and I do have someone out there, either in the End Realm or in the living world, that is without me and I them. I have no proof of this, yet in this moment I know. Something is telling the void in my chest and the space in my skull that I am bound with someone.

This all does nothing to budge my mood from the sudden depression that I'm trapped in—much like the black void around me—and still I remain motionless with the periodic addition of salt water hitting my lips, though now I at least do not wish for the end of myself. I've found escape from that at least, knowing that I still need to continue my efforts if not for myself, for the one waiting for my return.

The stone gives a jolting tremble beneath me as loud stammering scraping sounds begin to emanate from across the way opposite the corner that holds me up. I gather enough ambition to rotate my head toward the grinding just as hot orange light bursts forth, blaring and blinding my fully dilated eyes. A surge of warmth accompanies the newly risen light. It blazes across my left side, hell-bent on penetrating as far as it can. The audible scraping of stone cutting across stone continues, sending continuous quaking vibrations through the floor and walls into my bones. With my head against the wall, the strength of the quakes causes my jaw to bounce, smacking my teeth against each other.

The hot and bright emission shines through my eyelids as if I am looking into a planet's nearest star. Holding my hands up to help block some of the assaulting rays, I open my eyes ever so slightly to get a visual of what's happening and my surroundings—which up to this point have mostly evaded me. The light is two open flames of the natural orange-red fire color from the living world I have knowledge of, held in sconces the shape of large gargoyle-looking hands. One is ahead on the adjacent wall to my corner and the other on the parallel wall. What I recognize next sets forth the plague of insects that I so despise—the ones that eat at my innards.

My irises adjust to the newly bright conditions, and I can see what stone has been being cut and dragged across other stone. The room I'm in is a rectangular chamber of solid smooth slate. The far wall opposite me is slowly advancing itself, and this advancing wall that's causing the loud scraping noises and structural trembling is not smooth, but is riddled with sharp stalactite-like protrusions.

Pierce chamber . . .

In a mad rush of anxiety, it all makes sense in an instant.

The insects chew like a harsh wind ripping through my body, taking with it my organs, leaving me weightless, hollow, cold, but also pinned and chained to the hard surface beneath me. Fear doesn't just settle in during times like these; it devours.

It's clear now what is to happen. Gathering my mind, pulling myself out of the metaphorical chains that bite at and bind me, I run the few paces to the advancing piercing wall. I can see and feel just how sharp and erratic the spearing pattern of serrated stone is. Some spikes protrude from the wall by more than the length of my forearm, and others in the erratic pattern are much smaller, down to just a few inches in length. The wall moves at a slow pace. I only have to backstep every five or six seconds to keep from getting scathed by the wall's weaponry, but this brings me no comfort as this chamber is so very small. Looking back and forth between the two walls, I judge: less than a minute, maybe two . . . before this entrapment succeeds in its purpose.

There's absolutely no escape, and regardless of the forlorn state I was in just moments ago, I do not want to die. I need to get to where I promised I would be. I have to find a space in the pattern of the stone spears that will result in the least fatal damage to my body as possible. I scurry back and forth along the jagged shards, attempting to find the safest spot for me to get in position between the two walls. The vibrations start increasing in strength, rattling my legs and body even more as the wall begins to pick up speed.

Arhhh! Fuck-fuck-fuck! I'm running out of time . . . and fast. There's simply no spot along the wall that seems much better than another. The pattern of spikes is erratic, but there's no area of shorter spikes large enough for my entire body, even if I huddle myself up as much as possible, escaping being pierced by one or even several of the much larger stalactite spears is quickly deemed impossible, and I now have less than two feet of space to navigate between the flat wall and the other that's wielding its deadly slate spikes. There is no time. I am out.

About halfway between the center of the walls and the corner opposite the one that earlier safely housed me, I drop into a fetal position just in time to feel the first points of the wall pressing against me. My shoulder and just above my hip are where I feel it first, receiving sharp agonizing wounds. All I can do is sit here and clench my teeth together as hard as I can while I breathe heavily and scream in horrific agony through my viselike jaw. The wall doesn't even stutter at the meek resistance my body offers. I have no idea how thick these stone walls are, but my weight is laughable against their own.

The spike continuing its path through my shoulder scrapes its way across the inside of my collarbone. My vise can't hold—my jaw explodes in wails, indescribable wails, ones normally only heard in the worst of fictitious nightmares. Just when I think the pain can't get any worse, I'm hit with the shorter spikes of the wall. They team up and penetrate me all at once. It feels like rape from all directions. My breath escapes me, my lungs now shredded balloons, as the needle passing across my collarbone reaches the inner depths of my lower neck. Two spots crush against the side of my head, sending a harsh crack and shooting buzz across the inside of my skull, face, and down my spine.

A louder crack echoes like one of the stone spears has busted in half, but no, it's another damning fracture of my skull from the pressure.

I try to breathe. Nothing—lungs don't engage.

I try to scream. Nothing—silence.

I try to stay alive. Vision fades, and every sense dies away into darkness.

✪ ✪

I wake enough to hear a familiar heavy breathing and the heavy clops of hooves. The little vision I can achieve through the slits of my eyelids that seem impossible to spread is blurry and dizzying at best, yet I am able to make out the sight of a pair of legs approaching from a horizontal point of view as my face rests against the chilled slate floor. As I am dragged across the stone by my ankle, all I can think of is how I long to not fail my partner, to make it back to them. It is the first and only thing consuming my mind, like contagion, and it comes as a swarm of anxiety.

My head still buzzes with shooting sensations throughout my skull, the inner tissue of my brain, and down into my shoulders and spine. The pressurized feeling of my head being in a vise is a constant reminder of the fractures—the trauma caused by the closing walls of the chamber. Still being dragged, I have no energy, nor is my body in any shape to move in any manner. I catch a sudden glimpse of a glassy semi-translucent window, it's closing in on me as I'm dragged into it, first my knees are overtaken, then stomach, then chin. Abruptly blinded by an incredibly brighter white environment tells me I have been dragged through a portal like the one I previously encountered. The surrounding new air has a much less echoing and less stagnant audibility and wisp to it. It sounds and feels like I am now in a vast open area—comparatively anyway.

My leg's thrown out, let loose from the grasp that dragged me across the floor, allowed to land hard with no resistance from me, but no new pain is felt. Nothing is felt other than the leg's weight.

"This is the one I spoke of who bears the coins," barks a muffled and distant-sounding voice—like hands are placed over my ears or as if I am underwater.

Nothing's working correctly. I feel utterly broken, beyond repair, mentally and physically deceased. Not even my ears register or translate without major fault.

A light airy gasp is heard, sounding out in surprise. "What has happened to him? What have you done, brother?"

CHAPTER NINE

Tearmann

"**B**rother!" the light female voice projects with demand. "You *will* answer me."

"This soulless committed several crimes. The punishment received was fair and just."

I can barely move any part of my body due to the exhaustion I am in and the physical damage I have sustained. Still sprawled almost lifeless across the cold marble floor, my bony cheek with its full weight against the smooth yet harsh stone, I gather the energy to lift my eyelids enough to peer through the window-like slits. Vision is still slightly fuzzy, but I see a beautiful woman standing at the summit of a high staircase made of white marble veined in grays, and in front of me, slightly off to the right, is a heavy hoof that is unmistakably owned by Alastor of Chains—the coat of ashen hair and hock of his leg being further identifiers.

The woman starts descending the profound staircase. From what my vision allows me to see, she's of pure white complexion and wears a thin white dress that drapes loosely over her thin structure and feminine curves. The dress is so light and thin that it moves and folds elegantly in the still air just from her movement alone as she descends and approaches me and the warden. The dance of the silk is really the only reason I'm able to distinguish the white dress from her purest of white skin. As she takes her last steps to reach our location, I notice her bare feet and calves going in and out of view as her garment sways. Her skin, matte and powdery white, has no sign of blemishes, imperfections, or gradients at all. Her skin is as though she's been painted. She is beautiful and moves with a certain dignity and honor that brings me a feeling of enticing comfort.

"He is not even able to lift his head. Yet again, I question your judgment, brother."

"Just heal him and get this over with," Alastor barks. "I only brought him on account of his purse and his mention of your name. Apparently, the Maw divulged too much to this one."

"Pffft . . . please, Alastor."

"Roumph!" growls the warden at the woman's demeaning sarcasm.

"Do you aspire to higher levels of ignorance every time you visit?" she asks in spiteful rhetoric. "You know absolutely nothing of Karhon or little else outside your barren land of disgust."

At this point, I already know I am in the presence of Lunacrye. I am taken aback though by the fact I've been brought here by Alastor. Why? What's his reasoning for bringing me here? *Surely it was of his own will and choosing—or not? Ugh, I can't even fucking think straight.*

The warden scoffs again in a growl but offers no response to Lunacrye's obvious distaste for the demon.

"He needs to recover from the obscene situation you forced on his body and mind." Lunacrye comes down to meet me on the floor as she speaks and places a tender warm hand on my face. "He will stay in the sanctum under my care," she says, and Alastor rebukes her right away.

"He will *not!* This walker is soulless and is not to leave Tartarus or my imprisonment."

The warden gets hastily aggressive both with his volume and posture, his hooves positioning more dominantly. Lunacrye keeps her hand on my face though, remaining silent, her calm unprovoked by Alastor's disposition. She looks at me and I her through my still heavy eyelids. Her large sharp eyes are of pure glossy black with no whites, and in the middle of her forehead just above her two eyes is another eye of sorts, but this one is diamond-shaped and elongated vertically unlike the more typical shape of her main eyes. The contrast of her white skin and black eyes is beyond striking. Her face is just as white and seamless as her feet and calves. She has no hair, and her smooth face and forehead follow up into a crest the shape of a crescent moon, with the two points of the crescent facing up to the high ceiling and sky. Lunacrye looks as much alien as she does human, and she really is the absolute most beautiful thing I've seen or have any recollection of.

"He is here only because of his purse and—"

"Yes, brother!" Lunacrye interrupts in a shout as she darts her eyes from me to Alastor. "So I have *already* heard." She stands then, turning to face him. "I cannot perform any ritual with his truth coins while he is in this condition. This man will stay here, in the sanctum, under my care. If there is further issue with my ruling—"

"Rumpth. *Ruling?*" barks the warden.

"You seem to forget, dear—you traveled here, to my dominion. So yes, if there is further issue with my *ruling*, you can attempt to take your concern to Hades." She speaks softly and calmly other than the surprising spikes of spite and aggression toward Alastor. She seems both very in control of herself and also able to lose control if the right level of annoyance or disdain is reached.

Silence has fallen, and shortly, there is the awkward unknown language I remember from the moments before Rahkni shoved me through the portal summoned at the main wall. The warden has taken his leave.

The arch-sorceress comes down to me again, running the tips of her fingers across my jaw and past my chin. "You're safe here, human."

Lunacrye and I meet eyes again. I physically feel I cannot reply, though desire to meet her compassion with gratitude stirs in my heart. I'm just lucky enough to be alive and able to open my eyes some at this point. She stares at me, but I catch a glimpse of her third center eye blink with vertical lids.

"I will now spell you into a deep rest, where you can recover in peace. Please let go of any worry, dear human."

⬟ ⬟

I wake to an empty dimly lit room, where I lie on the floor covered well with a heavy thick fabric both underneath and over my body, which makes the hard marble floor a place of comfort. My eyes do not feel nearly as heavy, and I'm able to open them and look around with fair ease. It's a great relief to be able to lie here and move my head and neck. I feared the fractures of my skull may have caused some permanent paralysis or other lasting damage, but right now, this feels okay. A modicum of alleviation envelopes me. Any movement I make beyond that shows me my energy levels are still greatly sapped. The incredible pain I was in after the damage from the chamber has extinguished, and the agonizing buzzing through my nerves that was shooting around in my head and down my spine has gone away too. I wonder how long I have been recovering in this state of sleep. I bring a hand to my face and head where I sustained somehow death-defying injuries. Everything feels normal other than a hard patch of wrinkled scar tissue where I was pierced through the side of my head.

I bring myself up to sitting position while maintaining most of the fabric around me. Something about this situation feels like . . . home (whatever that even is; there is no recollection of a home or what that ever was or looked like for me before). Weak numbness tingles across me while I sit. Keeping my torso perched up takes some effort, but the fact there's no longer any of the heinous pain brings on a soft beach and gentle tide and an internal smile of such grandness, partnered with a cloud of deep indigo, ready though not willing to fell its hold.

The room is fairly large and overly basic in design. It's a marble room with an inordinately high ceiling. The marble is white, just like every other structure I have seen in the High Sanctum, and is veined with large geological roads of grays and tones of tan. It's just me and this large piece of warm fabric alone in this space, and in a way, it makes me think of a much more beautiful version of the pierce chamber.

The only structure within the room is a large window across the way. I look to it over my left shoulder. The large faceted shapes of smoke-stained glass radiate brilliance, cascading spectra onto the chamber's marble. This faint chromaticism bestows the room with dim ambient lighting, which aids in securing the feeling of home for me. I do not know what the skies look like in the Fields of Asphodel, but even if they are blindingly lit by a star like the skies of Earth, I would guess this room would still have this comfortable dim lighting that I'm blessed to bask in now. From the sinister pierce chamber to this empyreal stone home—the truest of dichotomies.

An archway is also cut in the wall behind me. It looks to lead to a hallway, one that's lit significantly brighter than here inside. There is no sign of Lunacrye or anyone else, and the airy silence doesn't give way to any audible disturbance. The urge to get up, cross through the archway, and seek an audience with the arch-sorceress is strong, as I want to be in her calming presence again. The thought comes to mind that she must really be able to help me get answers with the use of the truth coins. Alastor made it sound like the coins were one of the reasons for bringing me to the High Sanctum, and Lunacrye did mention that she must keep me here, as she could not perform the ritual with me in my previous state. What this ritual consists of, I haven't the slightest idea. Karhon nor anyone else has made mention of how the coins are actually used.

I decide to lie back down. This feeling of home and peace is so compelling. I had no idea this state of relaxation and contentment was ever possible. The ability to lay my head down on something other than a rucksack, rock, or hard ground is beyond inviting, and there does not seem to be any other logical option than to take advantage of this environment and rest my body within the weighted fabric. The lighting and escape of the archway still entices, so I rest in a way to face it, watching the only entry and exit of the room.

My eyelids grow heavy once more. I'm giving way, surrendering to the otherworldly plane of sleep. Just as the deep drag of that plane tries taking its final pull, a sphere crosses the entrance of the archway and comes to a stop, as if it has noticed me on the floor and halted its travel in surprise. It remains stationary as it floats in midair but makes quick sudden rotations in alternating directions. I feel as though it's focusing me, eying me up and scanning me in its own way. The orb looks to have a translucent glass-like encasement that holds three much smaller dark spheres suspended within a swirling fluid or possibly gas of white and beige. I remain in my prone position as I watch the sphere rotate back and forth in its focusing manner. Nothing about the sphere alarms me, and I feel content simply observing its nature.

Rotations stop abruptly, and the three internally suspended spheres make a quick change of pattern and position. They remain stationary after their sudden rearrangement. As the sphere slowly cuts through the still air in a direct path to my space on the floor, I sit up a bit, asking with intrigue, "And what are you?"

With this, the sphere diverts from its direct path and starts a more side-to-side slalom as it continues its approach. Then it comes to an easing stop, which happens to be a little too close for comfort at the altitude of my face. I back up some to kill the sense of personal intrusion. The sphere doesn't close the gap I've created.

"Sidus is the designation you wish to know," comes a genial female voice from the orb.

This definitely catches me off guard. I did ask the question aloud, but it was more out of general curiosity without directing the question at the spherical object specifically. I did not expect a response.

I give pause. "Are you sentient?"

"I am," the sphere affirms. "Both sentient and of mortal tissues. Well, to be exact, *was* of mortal tissues. My living days are over, just as yours are." My shock must be noticeable, as the sphere proceeds to add, "You're surprised by this," more in observation than question.

"I, uh . . . I am actually, yes."

To this, the sphere dives a little in altitude as it shifts its position to my right, ending its aerial suspension methodically at the same altitude it was prior to the short diving maneuver.

"You appear very . . . mechanical," I say with hesitation. "Forgive my candor. I mean no disrespect when I say this. You look like . . . You look almost manufactured."

The sphere responds, "The flesh and meaty life-forms that I am sure you are more accustomed to seeing are much easier for the universe to create, and therefore, I belong to a fairly rare branch of evolution. I take no offense at your words."

"Your outer structure looks of glass."

"It does," the sphere says. "I am made of a crystalline shell, highly composed of silica, though my internal structure is of deoxyribonucleic acid. So you see, you and I are much alike apart from the fact your species' genes lack the codons to bridge between carbon and silica."

"Hmm, I see. Simply a different instruction manual, then."

"Precisely," says Sidus. "Not only are you handsome, but also very intelligent. I like you," she says with cheerful enthusiasm, then adds in sneerful humor, "So far . . ."

"Ha!" The laugh is out loud, an irresistible impulse. "Are you hitting on me?"

"Obviously our species are biologically incompatible for procreation. Don't be silly. I am just being vocally observant. Plus, did it not feel good to hear such an observation?"

"It did," I answer, chuckling. "Thank you, Sidus."

"Sure thing, human," Sidus says, then takes an awkward pause as her three internal spheres all shift together up and to one side of her crystalline shell. "A-any-wa-ay, the arch-sorceress asked me to escort you to her dining area if you were awake on my arrival. You are awake, so let's go!" she says, again with that same cheerful enthusiasm.

Dining area? Like, food? I haven't seen a single food item since my arrival in the End Realm. In Tartarus, there are no such amenities, and food is something that has seemed nonexistent as well as pointless. The feeling of hunger has not plagued me, and there's no reason for nourishment here—our bodies seem to eternally sustain themselves somehow without such sources of intake.

Not wanting to look stupid, I decide not to question the dining and food topic. I make my way to my feet for the first time in—I'm not even sure really how long. Getting to a full upright posture brings a surge of loftiness, a slight otherworldly dizziness, as if this view from atop my shoulders is a new experience.

"Damn," I say, catching myself mid-sway. "How long have I been here recovering? I'll do my best. Hopefully I can walk okay."

"I am unsure how long you have been in the High Sanctum. A question for the arch-sorceress, I suppose."

I take a few strides, testing my capabilities.

"I would offer a hand . . ." Sidus says, and her three inner orbs peer my way—like how someone looks at you out the corner of their eye.

I chuckle a bit as I take a few more steps in trial. "Well, Sidus, I appreciate that, as well as your ability to get me to laugh. This place and its company have been a very different experience for me thus far."

"Shall we attempt this excursion now, fellow sentient being?"

"Yes, miss, let's."

The feeling of otherworldly dizziness remains, like I am relearning the sensation of controlling this vessel at such a high altitude. Lying down and relaxing feels familiar and of home, but standing up is something new at this moment.

Sidus leads the way through the archway and down the corridor. It is in fact much more lit down the hallway. The lighting does not falter regardless of how many turns, staircases, or rooms we proceed through, and there are many of each. The High Sanctum must be massive, and if it wasn't for my guide, I surely would be finding myself lost in this beautiful marbled maze. The lighting is ambient and has no source, no fixtures on the walls or ceilings. It's a magic or science that I can't begin to explain or hypothesize. Not knowing how certain things work is something I find irritating. I want to understand the laws and reasons behind everything I see, including seemingly simple things such as ambient lighting with no visible and tangible source—something I venture many people would not think twice about. It has my mind bothered the entire way to our destination.

Sidus and I come to another staircase, one I can finally see the top of with ease. This is a relief, as the others seemed irrationally long and just led on to more corridors and mostly empty rooms.

"This is where I take my leave." Sidus pauses a moment. "I never got your name, human."

"Ah, yeah, about that . . . I don't know my name." I give a resigned shrug. "Most just call me soulless or nameless." I offer a smile. "Human is fine too."

"That is a shame. I hope the rest of your day cycle goes well, human." With this, Sidus turns and disappears down the hall we came from, and I stand at the base of the short staircase.

Turning and looking back up the stairs, I wonder what is waiting for me and began the quick climb. The arch-sorceress stands from her position at a large central table in the room as I enter. The table is long and holds empty marble carved chairs, too many to count, on either side. The ends of the table each hold a single taller chair, the nearest one being that which Lunacrye has just stood up from.

"My dearest human," she greets as she walks to meet me, hands held out. "How do you feel?"

"Awkward, I would say. Being upright felt strange at first, but that is subsiding some, I believe. I feel no pain though! And my wounds seem to be healed," I say in relief.

"For that, I am glad. I can only imagine the pain felt from the injuries you sustained."

"Thank you so much for aiding me and allowing me to recover here," I say to Lunacrye as we stand facing each other, my hands resting in hers. Lunacrye is close to my height, her eyes just slightly above my own. I catch myself again noticing the beauty of her clean and powdery-looking skin. "I recognize if it were not for your help and care, I would either still be in a grave and dire state of health or quite possibly fully ended. Thank you so very much for—"

"You're welcome, dear," the arch-sorceress kindly interrupts and places a hand on my chest. "I would love for you to join me."

She turns and points to the chair at the end of the table that she had been sitting on, offering it to me. Something about having this chair offered to me, a soulless of Tartarus, by someone as high-ranking and important as the arch-sorceress of the Fields of Asphodel feels . . . backward. Though I do not want to question her or be the cause of any disrespect, and so I take the place at the end of the table.

Lunacrye chooses the chair nearest me on the left side of the marble table. "How long has it been since you have eaten?" she asks.

"Uh, I do not know how to answer that. I haven't eaten since my arrival at the gates. We do not get or need food in the lowest prisons." I raise my brow some. "And prior to that"—I take a deep breath—"well, I have no memory of the living world."

"I know that," Lunacrye admits. "I am able to see certain things about beings, places, objects even. That being said, unfortunately I never know what pieces I will get in my vision when I first see someone. It is very random."

"Can I ask?" I question as innocently as possible. "These random pieces you're able to see, is this the gift of your centermost eye?"

The sorceress curls her pale lips in a shallow smile. "This is what I have always assumed, yes. I am the only one of my kind, dear Jaesyk. One of the Originals of this realm. And so I have no others like me to ask if this is the truth, but I know it does not give me any typical vision like my other eyes do, so I have come to the conclusion that yes, the informative feeds I get when first seeing someone or something for the first time are likely the gift of the black diamond you see."

Curiosity about the Originals engulfs me, and the fact that the arch-sorceress is actually pleasant to talk with and gives much more sound replies than Karhon or anyone else I've encountered has me perked up and excited—in a good way, for the first time in . . .

Well, maybe this is a first.

"Are all of the Originals, as you say, one of a kind like yourself?"

"For the most part, yes."

"I overheard the conversation between you and Alastor on my arrival here. You are siblings but not of the same . . . species?" I ask. "Is that right?"

"Is it that obvious?" Lunacrye smiles wide and laughs as she sits back more in her chair. Again, I am caught off guard, enchanted—by both. Every new mannerism, movement, everything new I witness of her is uniquely stunning and beautiful. "We are siblings. It's hard to fully explain and even understand for us Originals, but we all know of each other on some level, and we have all been here since the beginning of time and space. Much like you and your lack of memory prior to reaching the afterlife, we know of nothing and have no memory of any universe prior to our creation."

"Wow, that's something I did not expect to hear. So something you knew since day one was that Alastor is your brother? What of your parents?"

"Yes, since the beginning, Alastor and I have known of our sibling bond. As for parents, none of us Originals really have parents, as you say. Hades is the creator of this realm and is a leader and guide to us all. He is not seen as a father or parent, however. He is seen as our leader and our god most of all."

"Did Hades create you and the other Originals, then?"

"That is where offering you facts becomes difficult." Lunacrye pauses for a moment, taking a slow breath. "To our knowledge, our existence began at the very same moment in time and space, including Hades's." She raises an open hand slightly off the table. "Anytime one of us has brought forth that very inquiry, he proclaims he does not know."

"Does that make sense?" I cut in. "If he was the creator of all of you, surely he would know."

Lunacrye giggles in jest and sits up from the lax position she took. "Yes, well, we settle for what Hades gives us. His presence and aura are both worthy and demanding of the highest degree of respect. It is not simple to explain, dear, but when your god shares his time with you, there is a precise way you present yourself, and this involves not questioning him."

"Although I have never been so lucky, I can begin to understand that. In a way, that is how I feel being honored with your company."

"That is kind of you to say." Lunacrye lowers her crescent head to me some in a bow, then looks back to me. "In my mind," she says, "I am no more important than you and you no more than I. Now!" she exclaims with both wrists shooting out, hands pointing outward. "Let us enjoy some fruit together, my dearest Jaesyk."

Fine stone plates and bowls quickly come into form near us on the table in a vaporous way. After the stoneware solidifies, various fruits of all colors make their way into existence, filling the plates and bowls in the same vaporous-like fashion. As amazing as this magic is to see, I have only one thing on my mind.

"Arch-sorceress, that is—"

She shakes her head side to side in a correcting manor. "No, call me Lunacrye. Please."

"Okay." I nod and accept timidly. "So, I heard you say that before and didn't understand. I just figured it was over my head." I chuckle at myself a bit. "But what is a jaesyk? Are you calling *me* that?"

"Mm-hmm. One of the pieces my oculus gave me. That is your name, dear human." She meets my eyes and gives a playful wink with her left. "Now, let's eat!"

A small plate is passed across the marble table closer to me. It wields strawberries, green grapes, and a black berry I'm unfamiliar with. I decide to try the strawberries first.

CHAPTER TEN

Remittance

I lay back in the sanctuary of the bare marble room with the heavy weighted fabric around me. My mind's racing through the events of the day. Both gratitude and sadness swell as I navigate all the emotions and information that I have gained.

The arch-sorceress bestowed much on me. I now know my name, though the name Jaesyk doesn't trigger any past recollection, and the name itself feels awkward and foreign, I still find a sense of relief in knowing this newfound piece of me. A name helps me feel closer to being whole and knowing who I am. Something as simple as knowing one's own name—everyone takes that for granted down here, as it's one of the most basic of personal identifiers one can have. I could never blame them. Hell, I would've taken it for granted as well. Though I never complained or divulged to anyone the hurt and frustration of such things. Not knowing my name and being alone, being known as "Nameless"—it has in fact been a source of pain. Already feeling lost and alone in most ways imaginable, not having the most basic source of self-identity was generally a daily disturbance. I am thankful this pain is now one of the past.

As we shared the conjured fruit, no void in my stomach was filled. The fruits were delicious. This was the first time my sense of taste had been of any importance in the afterlife, but there was no fulfillment in the sense of hunger. Nonetheless, the sweet tastes of sugars and acids they contained were enjoyable. They brought on small surges of saliva with each hit of their sourness, and they brought on the urge for memories too—memories of who else I had shared times like this with, and if I had a favorite fruit, which fruit was it?

Lunacrye and I made conversation around the truth coins and the ritual needed to make use of the coins. I asked to know more about her, as she was very captivating to me, and we also discussed my experience in the End Realm so far. She was very willing and enthusiastic in answering any questions I had about her and her life. I learned of her love for watching over the Fields of Asphodel and caring for its inhabitants. I could tell Lunacrye takes great pride in making the fields a place of beauty, from the fields of lush grasses and flowering gardens she told me of to the large dwellings she builds to specification for each newcomer to the fields. Regardless of their species or the number of family members, the arch-sorceress makes the needs and desires of her population a priority. It was inspiring to see someone so committed and happy helping facilitate others' happiness. In ways, it gives me further validation and encouragement that the journey I find myself so committed to isn't foolish at all, as long as it's the path I want to be on and desire.

I have all of this and so much more on my mind since Sidus took her leave after escorting me back, when really, the one thing I should be focusing on is the question I am to pose in the truth coin ritual. And my time with this is limited, as Lunacrye had told me we would be performing the ritual tomorrow. Lunacrye explained the ritual to me in depth and also helped me understand more about the coins themselves. She kindly explained that truth coins are only bestowed on souls that own a worthy heart, that they are extremely rare, and when they *are* seen, they are typically held by souls that enter the afterlife with access to the Fields of Asphodel or even the Elysium Halls. She said this is why me entering the realm with them was so extraordinary and "wrong" to a certain degree. She agreed that a soul bound for Tartarus should not have entered the End Realm with such coins. They are considered a grand gift, as even in the afterlife, most souls still have unanswered questions about the universe or some other aspect of existence that they don't feel they got answers to while alive and now in death, still wish to know. Truth coins are gifts generally used in attempt to get those answers, those truths.

The success of the ritual has much to do with how well I construct the question I want answered. The arch-sorceress explained there are clever ways to trick the ritual so the possessor of the coin can receive answers to more than one question, if the question is crafted in such a covert manner. I have much to think about. I have to figure out what my priority is. Is my priority learning more about my past or my next step in reclaiming my memory? Is my priority learning of a way to escape the End Realm? Both these avenues are ones of desire, though really what I want most is information about my spouse.

"And if I have one," I say aloud for no one to hear.

I know I was done questioning this (if I truly am wedlocked or not), and I *do* feel it inside me. I feel the truth. I know it to be true. But I still have no hard evidence, so the logical man in me can't refute that there's a chance my intuition is wrong. My main reason for escaping the End Realm though is the drive to find my partner, and the main reason why I want my lost memories is to have more information on this person. It's clear that the most logical direction of the ritual then should be seeking a way to find out if I have a spouse and where they are. If I am to find out I'm not wedlocked to another, then my entire mentality and direction in this afterlife could change. If I find out that I in fact am, then I will absolutely continue headstrong on my current quest. *This ritual is my chance at hard evidence, a final way to throw that damned looming question away for good.*

After sharing my story with Lunacrye, she made very clear in a strong and serious tone that she would only perform the ritual once with me. The arch-sorceress stressed heavily that Hades's limits are boundless as far as what he can achieve with a truth coin versus what she ever could, and though she mentioned that the chance of me ever being in his presence is astronomically implausible, she made direly clear that if I were to ever get out of the End Realm, it would be the Devil-God's doing. No one else has that power. It feels imperative that I keep one of my truth coins reserved for this astronomical implausibility.

I have spent likely over an hour thinking hard about what my question should be for the ritual. The simplicity of the question that keeps coming back to me is *so* simple that it has me second-guessing myself, and so I keep pushing that one aside and trying to focus and think harder—deeper—pushing for a question far more complex and therefore better. One not so simple.

Goddammit. I'm complicating this far too much. Or am I?
Fuck. I don't know.

My frustration echoes off the walls of what *was* a silent room. I just feel this question I keep coming back to is far too simple for what Lunacrye said about cleverly constructing a question to trick the ritual into answering more than one. Frustration ricochets once more, and fingertips grip the scalp hidden below my forest of hair. *Yup, fuck it. I'm fighting this too much, and I'm done overcomplicating it. This question, if answered, will give me the information that is most vital to me at the moment. So that's that, damn it.*

Now, feeling confident about the result of my quest for the perfect question, the weight and anxiety of wanting to find such perfection has fallen. Mental peace comes, taking me to a place far away from previous ruminations. In this place, I am met with ease and silence. In this place, I can sleep, and so I allow the heft of my eyelids its victory.

✦ ✦

Sidus is suspended just a short distance from my face and elevated from my still prone position of sleep. She has such a vast variety of movements, but at the moment, she looks to be fairly static. Only her crystalline shell is rotating and in a much less erratic fashion than when we first met, when she had appeared to be focusing and evaluating me with quick rotations in randomized directions. This time, she is rotating slowly, and the rotations are changing direction in a smooth and gradual manner.

I blink a few times to aid in further waking from my slumber and so my eyes can discern her more sharply.

"Oh!" Sidus jumpily exclaims, almost as if she has been startled. "I did not become aware of your status change, err like, until just now. That is . . ." she rambles as she exits her static stationary position and begins floating more loose and casually.

I sit up, letting out a progressively overbearing yawn, rubbing and ridding my eyes of the sleep they are so reluctant to let go of.

"So, um, how long have you been awake, human?"

I don't want to stop massaging the sleep away, but I know there won't be an end to it unless I force my hands from my eyes. I battle it, and my hands fall to the fabric over my thighs. I look over at Sidus. She has already raised herself to my new level of height since my posture change.

"Like, did you just wake up? Just now?" She speaks fast compared to how I normally hear her, and the awkward gaps between her quick ramblings are easy to note. "Or . . . maybe you were awake and aware of my presence for some time?" she adds in a slower and reluctant, almost fearful way. I also notice she has done that thing again where all her internal orbs are bunched up and to one top corner quadrant of her sphere.

"Huh?" I ask. "What are you talking about? I just woke up now and sat up. Didn't you see?"

She veers to her right so that she's more directly in front of me rather than off to my right side. "Well, yes. I mean, I know you just now woke up—just—just never mind is all. I was just verifying the time of your status change."

"Uhhh, oookay . . ." I drag out, confused. "But how long were you here?" I turn my head to the side a bit while still looking her way. "Were you watching me sleep, Sidus?"

I chuckle a bit, and Sidus's inner orbs, still bunched up, start gently bumping into each other up in their corner. "Well, so what if I was?" she says both playfully and aggressively while kind of darting toward me a bit, finally letting her inner spheres loose from their position of embarrassment.

I laugh more heartily at this as I reply, "Well then, I would say that is a little fuckin' weird, Sidus!" And I smile at her to show I'm being humorous and not confrontational.

She giggles some more and admits, "Well, there is no argument there!" Sidus is loftier and freer as she traverses the air now.

"You're fucking hilarious. Thanks for the awkward experience this morning, ya goof."

"Aw, human. If I had utility appendages, I would have to hug you now," she says, still laughing.

"Hey! That reminds me, you don't have to call me human anymore. Lunacrye was able to tell me my name. It's Jaesyk."

"Hmm." Sidus starts casually floating around the room. I can tell her inner spheres are no longer looking my way while she loops around contemplatively. "Nope. I like human better. I mean, if you prefer I call you by your newfound name, then I will respect such request, but . . ." She's back around now, close and looking at me. "What can I say, I like calling you human!"

"Well then, that is just fine." I can't help but laugh while talking with this creature. She is just so damn fun and easygoing.

"Just you though. Only you can get away with addressing me so informally." I roll my eyes to add to the jest.

Sidus somehow completely ditches her normal voice and uses a generic human tone. "Well, fuck. That just makes me feel so goddamned special now, doesn't it?" She stops dead in her tracks, peering my way. "From what I've gathered from studying you, I believe this to be a casual yet somewhat snide response written in your tongue," she says in her normal feminine voice. "How did I do?"

Again, I find myself naturally laughing. I'm joyfully amazed and surprised by her sense of humor, as well as her ability to pick up on my idiosyncrasies so accurately after such a short amount of time knowing each other. "Yes, that is damn near fucking spot-on!"

We both share in the lightness of the air and conversation for a few seconds longer, then she jostles midair like she's shaking herself from the playfully lax tone. "All right, so today is big, human. Have you thought of what you will ask during the truth ritual?"

"I have. I know exactly what I will ask. When will I meet with Lunacrye to get started?"

"I was told that is a decision you will need to make. I can escort you to Lunacrye as soon you'd like."

"Fuck it. Let's go now."

✹ ✹

Lunacrye sits opposite me, cross-legged on the marble floor. The room we're in is much different than any other location I have previously seen in the High Sanctum. The dozens of varying sized candles make the darkness of the room waver with a soft amber glow that creeps across the room like a vampiric shadow. The ambiance has me feeling pricks, scratches across my arms and shoulders that I know are not really there. My eyes keep checking areas where the amber doesn't reach—the same areas over and over again, just in case. Many of the larger candles supply the atmosphere with steady soft illumination; smaller-diameter candles cast off in ire, giving a flickering pulsating cadence of light that makes some of the features of the room bounce in and out of view. The high sections of massive stone columns and pilasters running each side of the longer walls and decorative molding at the ceiling are such features. Everywhere else I have been in the arch-sorceress's castle has been well lit, simple, and cleanly designed. Where we are now is still made of the beautiful white-and-veined marble just as the rest of the castle, but the extravagance and intricacy of the architecture here is very polar to that.

In this darkness, Lunacrye looks much different. Her physical aesthetic becomes inherently wicked within the dim flames of amber birthed from the candles as they drip their wax, almost as though the darkness has brought corruption to her. If not for already knowing her compassion, in this darkness, I would likely no longer feel in the presence of nurture and safety. Our silence only adds to this air of sinister gloom, and though I do enjoy the well-lit and almost angelic nature of the rest of the High Sanctum, there is always something about a dim and dark atmosphere that feels comfortable. I seem to find a certain beauty in darkness where others here in the End Realm often feel unease. I have come to realize and respect this as a characteristic that makes me, me. Here though, now, in this eerie ambiance, I feel unease fighting against that comfort.

There are few candles within our proximity, but enough warm light from the countless others throughout the occult room reaches us for me to effectively take action and begin the ritual. It is important that the ritual room remain quiet and focused, with focus being given only to the question and the payment at hand.

I sit up from the buffer of heavy fabric between the cool stone floor and me, while Lunacrye remains completely motionless in her perfectly straight posture. She has become so committed and peaceful in her meditative state that for a moment, while I smooth the truth coin I've chosen between my thumb and fingers, I am reminded of Karhon of the Rivers—his mannerism of suddenly becoming so completely inanimate that you questioned if time itself had frozen and only you existed alone in a world of timelessness. The feminine power sitting before me may well be just as blind as the Maw, for all three eyes remain peacefully closed so no contrast is to be seen on her gorgeous face of pale powdery white.

I begin to question, as I stand in the soft warm cadences of flame, Karhon's heeded words. *Do not ever lose or barter thy truth coins.* The Maw's advice plays in my head as I continue to massage the embossed pentagrams on the golden coin. For a reason unknown and intangible to me, I realize that I still hold more trust in Karhon than even the arch-sorceress, and a sudden wave of distrust and questioning abrades across me. Alastor, who I have zero reason to trust, brought me here to his high-ranking sister because I have truth coins, which are valuable, to say the least. Was this a ploy? Is Lunacrye's caring disposition one of manipulation? Is this all a ruse to get me to hand over my coins?

Argh, this is not the time or place for such a distracting possibility. But maybe I don't hold as much trust in Lunacrye as I thought. I stop smoothing the truth coin between my fingers and clutch it firmly in my palm, remembering. *I trust the Maw though, and it was he who told me, "I only know of two who could possibly offer the truths."* That gritty low voice of the monster I met clearly replays in my head—impossible to forget such a thing. On top of this rhetoric, I also have to remember everything I *do* know of the arch-sorceress is compassion, acceptance, care, and love. I do have reason to trust her too.

Push this uncertainty shit aside, man. Now is not the time to be questioning this. If this all pans out to be a manipulation, then deal with it when it comes. Right now, trust Karhon's words and stick to the path, stick to the ritual, and hope for the answers you seek. Don't fuck this up.

I breathe. I walk forward with a light foot and calm ease. Nothing about this is to be rushed or done haphazardly. Calm, focused, slow, and methodically, I lower myself to Lunacrye's level as she silently sits, still cross-legged with her hands resting on her fair calves. Letting her know of my approach, I gently place a hand on hers. She moves not a muscle other than slightly opening her mouth for me to place my chosen coin. After resting the coin on her tongue, her lips meet again, and I quietly take my place opposite her on the floor.

It does not take long for the water in the cauldron between us to start writhing with a shallow boil. The absence of fire beneath the cauldron makes it hard to see much more than its silhouette. The dim candlelight only aids the water in evading my sight, though the audible roiling is evidence enough of the ritual's progression. I stoop forward some to grasp the raw quartz crystal I chose the evening before. Lunacrye took me to a room filled with stones, gems, and crystals of all types and sizes. Out of the vast collection, I was to choose one that spoke to me the strongest, and something about this raw, untouched, and unpolished clear shard of quartz with its deep maroon hematite inclusions along its length instantly drew me in. Although I can't say that it "spoke" to me, as Lunacrye worded it, out of the entire room of mineral formations, this is the one I felt I had to leave the room with.

With the ambient writhing in the cauldron, I focus my mind on the somewhat rough shard of hematoid quartz gripped tightly in my left hand and on the question I seek to be answered. My mind takes its time, discarding all else, becoming so enamored with just those two that I become unaware of how much time has passed while doing so. My question replaying over and over in my head, focusing on the answers I wish to receive, I pour all my energy into taking that question from my mind, grasping the essence, extracting it. I imagine feeling it pass down my shoulder, past my elbow, into my wrist, and finally, confidently sealing it away into the vessel through the iron grip I hold it with.

Confidence is the destination I have come to. I know the energy of my question is now encapsulated in the quartz shard, and so when I hear the crystal joining the water in the caul-dron after letting loose my grip, a wave of relief falls over me. The relief of knowing and believing I have succeeded in this important step. A step that I honestly previously felt unsure of and anxious about, as I had concern over even believing such a thing was possible.

Kneeling down on the fabric feels right this time rather than sitting cross-legged. I don't even get a chance to get all the way down and situated before the room rushes to black, with a strong wind smashing the amber flames of the candles down into darkness. The rush of air has no sustain, it dies just as fast as it came to fruition. Within the pure silence of dark-ness, a sudden deep and drawn-out gasp of breath comes from Lunacrye, sounding almost mildly painful, like that of someone who has held their breath underwater for far too long. An urge to run over to her position in aid races through me, but I stop myself. It's far too dark to make my way around the cauldron and candles amongst the floor, and I know the repercussion of disrupting the ritual.

Slowly, the flames of the candles gradually become reignited, though not all at once. The candles relight in a sweep around the room much like the hands of a clock traversing their path in time. The warm candle glow makes Lunacrye again visible and even more corrupted-looking than before. She still sits cross-legged, but now the arch-sorceress is slightly lunged for-ward, her back strongly arched and her chin tilted toward the ceiling of the room with her jaw spread open. Again, I have the desire to aid her. She looks as though a massive hand has hold of her entire spine, torquing it in an excruciatingly sadistic grip of control. She's completely inanimate and silent in her marionette-like posture, all three of her obsidian black eyes wide open. A beam of soft white light starts slowly protruding from her hinged mouth, where a slight gleam of gold diffracts from the placed coin.

The protruding light beam keeps rising until it reaches a few feet from its source, ending in soft diffusion. The truth coin begins to rise from the resting place of Lunacrye's mouth, slowly flipping as it rises through the path of the beam.

"The truths I so seek," I say aloud as I kneel on the floor, keeping my gaze on my payment as it floats through the protruding light, "I cannot find. And so, universe, I pay thee and ask . . ."

The coin reaches near the end of the beam, where its spin slows and starts dissolving from view as though it's breaking down on the molecular level. The particles of the golden coin spread out, dispersing through the end of the diffused and dying beam of light as if there is a source of gravity in that void of space.

"Where is my spouse?" I ask, bringing finality to my incantation.

This is as far as Lunacrye went with me in explaining the ritual. Reciting the incantation and asking the universe to answer my question and accept my payment were the progressions the arch-sorceress drilled me on over and over again because all of that is direly important, and done wrong in the slightest way would surely mean the ritual failing. Not knowing what is to come next brings me excitement and a flurry of nerves. Excitement at the prospect of such desired answers and anxiety from the fear of not knowing if I have succeeded in my part of the ritual.

The protruding light dims to nonexistence, and the arch-sorceress's body leaves its inanimate state. Her two main eyes close as she shakily sits up—straighter but still postured as a marionette.

She looks as though the massive spectral hand grasping her spinal cord still reigns, owning a puppeteer's control of her.

Her oculus remains wide as she speaks in a strained and awkwardly constricted voice. "Your spouse, Nahla . . ." Her voice is just barely recognizably her own, strained and slow. She breathes raspy drawn-out gasps as she readies each of her next phrases. "In a hospital, on the celestial body known as Earth . . . located in the Orion Spur of . . . Via Lactea."

Her last word doesn't seem to end. Its pitch holds and trails off as the flames in the room fight hard to remain lit against another sudden, though calmer wave of wind that circles the room rather than pushing through as a crushing blast. With the flames fighting for their continued existence on their wicks, the room darkens enough that I lose sight of Lunacrye, and the held note from her last spoken word is stomped out just as my visual of her is stolen.

Candlelight becomes steady again with the departure of the winds, which I have now recognized as the universe in which I've given remittance to. I can see an arch-sorceress that is now in full control of herself, no longer a marionette. Taking a moment, we meet each other's eyes through the amber glowing darkness . . . eventually giving way to mutual victorious smiles.

CHAPTER ELEVEN

Fields

Shortly after the completion of the ritual, Lunacrye walks me through her maze of marble. The massive ebony wood cathedral doors that eventually come into view make my shoulders slump and head hang a touch. I know what this means. I'm so torn. Part of me definitely wants more time in the comfort I have been in here and to learn more about Lunacrye and Sidus. Hell, I haven't even said goodbye to that flirtatious and awkward crystalline orb I came to befriend so quickly. Lunacrye ushers me out with haste before I have much of a chance to debate, saying, "My dear, you must go. You have someone very important to get back to. I wish you the best of luck, dear Jaesyk."

And she's right. I do have somewhere else to be, someone to be next to. And damn, I have really no clue how I am going to get there. But I have to keep moving and keep to my goal of getting to her, the person I belong to, Nahla.

The hug the arch-sorceress gives me as the ebony double doors open for my departure wraps up well who Lunacrye is and how pure her heart is . . . as long as you aren't on her bad side, that is—like Alastor, evidently. Needless to say, I will greatly be missing Lunacrye, Sidus, and the High Sanctum. It is the closest thing to a home I have any memory of.

I step through, and the cathedral doors slam behind. Echoes of the Deliverance Gates charge at me. My jaw drops not from the charging memories, but from the breathtaking vista laid out in its grandness all around. I am miles above magnificent fields below. Miles and miles of golden grass fields, some of them flowering elegant white throughout the mass basin below, spread as far as I can see to a horizon that seems unfathomable to ever reach. Clusters of homes that make up villages dot the fields of white asphodel flowers like anthills across a vast acreage. A gentle breeze swifts through my hair and over my skin. This high up, it must be invisible dancing dragons, entities of wind, because only gods and dragons live at such heights.

I take my first steps down the seemingly never-ending staircase of glittering black marble, the only harsh contrast of the castle I've seen. The beauty of this awe-striking landscape makes me forget my desire to stay within the white walls, and for a while, as I walk the stairs, I am escaped, escaped from any thought at all. I am in the dragons' breeze and the solace of this place. This heaven.

The descent is long, and Nahla enters my thoughts. Her name—I wish it struck a memory for me, but it doesn't. A heavy sigh comes forth, one brought on by bittersweetness. I'm beyond grateful to know it though (her name, that is). It's pretty, and it leaves me longing to know the face it is matched with. The arch-sorceress said the name is feminine and carries with it a meaning "strongest of will, heart, and mind." So I now too have fair reason to believe my spouse to be a woman—something I can't help but feel most of the souls below in the fields wouldn't think twice about, though for me, any bit of information about who I am or who Nahla is feels significant, like the heaviest riches in the world.

I start reminiscing on the ritual. I think of how Lunacrye almost seemed just as excited and happy about the outcome as me. She was adamant that many pieces of information did not *have* to be given in answer to the question I posed. My spouse's name, for example, was fairly abstract from what I asked and an added piece I should be very thankful for (which I absolutely am). She seemed confident that we received so much because of how well the ritual was performed and how much power of heart I poured into the exchange.

My eyes go to the big skies, so different this place is from the areas I've seen thus far. The sky is bright blueish orange, and tall thunderhead clouds cruise the openness as if they are giving a slow but dedicated chase to something that goes unseen. Godly rays of orange subjugate the deep blue hues of the thunderheads. There is a war in the sky. The cool and warm hues fight each other for dominion. The warm godly rays do everything they can to reach and illuminate the fields below. It's magnificent.

I slow my descent as calm fire spreads across my face, blinding me some. My hand acts as a shield against the holy ray of light as it brings me to center stage. From under my shield, I peer into the source above. Not one, but two stars crest over one of the titanic clouds. *Two suns. Amazing. Damn, this place is gorgeous. I wonder if they're real . . . Is this how beautiful the afterlife is for some? This is more a dream than it is death.*

The last glittering black stair is partially overgrown with golden brown field grasses. I half turn around, peering over my shoulder, my neck craned to the target. The sheer altitude of the High Sanctum makes its details blur, as if there's a mist amongst the heights. I close my eyes, my gaze at the summit becoming blind.

Thank you.

I hop off the last stair. The soft crunch of field grasses just barely permeates the ambient chorus of tall golden wheat singing in the constant winds. Not a scent of sulfur to be found; instead, earthen smells treat my nose. Smells of life and freedom. A new wind brings a sudden hint of sweet pollen. It beckons me, and I allow the pull. It's better I head this way anyway—opposite the direction of Tartarus. I have no idea what it all entailed, but Lunacrye made clear to me not to worry about Alastor or his officers, telling me *not* to head back toward the prison, that she would handle the situation and for me not to question her on it. She too mentioned to do what I can to hide the three of swords branding atop my hand, as the sight of the soulless mark would bring concern to almost any outside of the prison's walls. This is something I need to stay mindful of, as I currently have no way of covering it. I look down at the evidence of my damnation. *Gloves . . . gloves would be nice.*

A few miles through the golden wheat, the sweetness on the air becomes more saturated. Eventually, I am on a thin trail leading into striking white asphodels that put an abrupt border and end to the brilliancy of the golds behind. I spread my arms out low, just above my hips, as I follow the trail. The field is so concentrated with the flowers that I feel I'm wading through a shallow ocean of frothed pearls. The winds gently dance them in swirls of choreography. I look down from the endless view of white to watch my hands pass through the canopy of petals, their silk brushing across my palms. Coerced pollen billows from my encouragement into saffron clouds, leaving a wake of yellow-orange on the trail.

A distant giggle breaks me from the euphoria. Ahead, cresting the tops of asphodels, I can see the emergence of homes. I let my scarred hand fall closer to my thigh under the blanket of white as I near.

The dense asphodels gradually fade into low meadow, where the sight of homes is soon accompanied by a crowd of voices from deeper within, smashed together like the bustling of a market square. A lone little girl giggles. She's chasing a ball through the low grasses while holding a single cone of picked asphodel high at her fragile shoulder. She meets the ball again with a haphazard kick, taking notice of me and loosing another giggle in her childish pitch of glee.

"Oh!" she says. Her smile gets bigger. Warm rays dazzle off her shiny round eyes. "Here, catch!" She skips, meets the ball again, and gives it another awkward send with her tiny bare foot. The ball is wide to my left, but an instinct in me has me surprisingly jumping for it—outstretched and hands out farther than I thought possible, as if the world's fate rests on me preventing the ball falling to the meadow floor. I crash to the ground hard, the low grasses offering far littler aid from the impact than I wished midair.

Fuck . . .

I groan, tweak my neck up toward my hands. *Ha! Got it.*

She giggles. "Di that hurt? Good catches!" She skips over.

"Nah, the grass broke my fall. Didn't ya see?" I sit up, kneel, brush myself off. "Here's your ball, little one."

"Oouu." Her brow scrunches, no giggle. "Di that hurt?" She grabs her ball and lets it fall to the grass while she points at my hand.

Fucking Christ, man. You've been made by a six-year-old.

"Ah, yeah . . . That one *did* hurt. I don't like people seeing it—"

"My name's Gemma!" She bursts through, then holds her hands with her flower cone to her navel, rotating her hips back and forth. "Do you like the flowers?" She nods to the pearl sea behind me. "They're my faverit. My mum's too. I pick her some e-every day. I wish I could pick some for Da."

I chuckle a bit. "I do like them, little one. There are so many. It's almost unbelievable."

She shows her big joyous smile again and rotates more at her hip. "Yeah, unbeliev-bul!" Her happiness is radiant, feeling almost tangible.

"So why not pick some for your dad? Is he not a flower guy? Surely he would love some from you, kiddo."

"Mum says one day, but he isn't here yet."

My stomach sinks, fades, goes cold. Gemma's aura made me forget. *She's dead . . . Shit,* I'm *dead. But she's like six and such a sweet thing . . .*

A childish vigor that awakened in me, brought to light by this little girl, is now at war with a sour melancholy that is trying to rise in power, much like the warm and cool hues in the skies above us. I feel pity for her, for dying at such a young age—something no soul this young would deserve—and for her missing her father. Though, from seeing her smile and spirited playfulness, I also can't help but think, maybe the living worlds are more of a hell than the afterlife is.

I find my chin more near my chest than before. "Ah, I see. I'm sorry, kiddo. I'm sure he wishes he were here with you."

"Hey," she says as tiny soft fingertips come under my chin while I'm looking at the ball in the grass. "Don't be sad. He's coming! Mum said so! I'm gonna give him the biggest hug too!"

I look up and give her a big smile. It's hard to not match her spirit, feeling as though any war sadness or anger would try to wage within her air would surely meet impossible odds.

"Make me a deal, kiddo?"

"Mm-hmm!" She nods exaggeratedly. "What is it?" She giggles.

"Make sure you give him a cone of flowers, just like that one, when you give him that biggest hug. Okay?"

"Okay!" She nods more and smiles. "But only if you catch the ball o-one more time, cuz deals have two sides, ya know." Her smile fades into pursed lips and a raised eyebrow, hustling me for more play.

I chuckle and put my hand out to shake. "Deal!"

Gemma giggles, swipes up the ball, and darts away, leaving me hanging. Her giggles turn to laughs as she drops the ball to the meadow floor, kicking it a few times to put more distance between us.

"Hey now, let's try to kick it closer to me this ti—" *Shit.* The ball is sent with joyous hearty laughs roaring from behind it that have both of Gemma's hands on her belly. I run. I calculate. I leap. I grab the ball. *Haha! I got it!* Then I crash to the ground again, hard. I do what I can to hide the groan.

"Oooo!" she lets out, but it's more of a shaped laugh than it is a sympathy.

I get up, laughing as I brush myself free of grasses. "*Now* it's a deal!" I point at her, smiling.

"Yup! Deal's a deal." Giggles ensue.

"It was nice meeting you, kiddo. I'm off now, okay?"

Gemma is already playing again, too busy to reply, kicking the ball and skipping around, but I catch a last glance from her and a smile as I walk away.

I head deeper into the bustling, passing many types of buildings and homes as I go. And I can't escape the thought: *I really hope that man isn't bound for Tartarus.*

✪ ✪

Fresh fruits and vegetables, bread, an array of different pollens—all scents on the air that strike my nose as I close in on the volume of smashed-together voices. Many smooth dirt pathways crisscross and become wider the farther in I go. Many walkers cross my path, most offering a greeting, whether it be a smile and nod or cordially spoken word. I am caught a bit off guard by the polarity of such demeanor and that of the other walkers I've met over the last year. There were no smiles in the Lowest and generally no cordial greetings either.

I round a corner between two homes, one made of wood and the other laid stone, though not as measured and neat as modern brick. The rumbling of hundreds of voices cuts crystal clear, no longer muffled in my ear. Walkers are everywhere, some weaving in and out, while others move with the calm of mature patience. Tents, stands, and tables spread across the village center with a full wheel of colors, tones, textures, even moods.

Ting, ting, ting.

The piercing ring catches me from the edge of the market and sixty yards or so farther in from where I stand as a blacksmith strikes to shape their current piece. Pots, pans, knives, and other tools hang and sway gently on a nearby rack—the smith's wares. A woman with blond hair wearing a beige dress steps near the smith and shows him a metal cooking pan. He holds his forging hammer to the side, taking a break from his next swing, and nods to a wooden barrel, which the woman tosses her pan into. Two children much younger than Gemma rush out of the crowd to her as she steps to the rack of wares. The kids jump and point at different pots and pans. The woman is only looking at one though, and she plucks it from the rack, raises a hand, and shouts something to the smith over her shoulder. She rounds up the two children (one of them clearly more obedient than the other) and proceeds deeper into the market. She is fast lost to me within the fray.

Observing from this distance feels awkward. I feel I'm being watched, spotted, examined. I do not want to look so solitary; blending more seems wise. I do well to hide the top of my hand as I march closer, joining the bustling population of the market. It seems to never end: the tents, stands, racks, and tables of goods and produce. The gamut of colors and scents is damn near overwhelming, yet alluring, and seems to excite me in a way that reminds me I'm human. I hear couples conversing about dinner plans and what items they'll need, children pleading for a new wooden toy or a certain fruit they spot, someone asking the owner of a jewelry stand if they can design a custom necklace, to which they say, "Surely. What beads were you thinking?"

I harness my nerves and collect enough initiative to approach a male walker scanning bins of tomatoes for his preference. His ears are sharp as serrated leaves, his cheekbones sculpted like mountain ridgelines, his eyes beady and bulbed.

"Excuse me, sir."

"Aye? Finest of a day as always, innit?" He glances me over as he talks, but his hunt continues—hand in the tomato bin, eyes investigative.

"It really is. Say, I don't mean to be a bother, but I was wondering if there's a place to get—this may sound weird—clothing around here? Specifically looking for a pair of gloves."

The walker stands taller, taking his face out of the hundreds of red orbs, and looks me over again. I might as well be a tomato now. "New here, aye?"

I squirm a bit. "Gah, admittedly, yes."

"Eh, don't ye sweat it. New walkers every day, of course."

A wash of minor relief flows. "I'm sure it gets easier. Just feeling a bit lost right now though."

"No worries, mate." He bats his hand through the air at me. "So, the square here is always active, and vendors come and go throughout the daylight hours. We all contribute to the village in our own ways, some little, some lots, so whatever ye need, in most cases, ye can find it here in the square. There are several tailors in the village, but I think right now the only one out is Harra." He points across the way, farther in. "His stand is just over that way, past a few of the apple sellers."

"That's a huge help. Thanks."

"Aye, and if ye have any questions, ask anyone—no dark souls here to worry about."

I nod and leave for the tailor's stand, a little hurried from the thought that maybe the walker somehow pegged me as one of those "dark souls."

Making my way through the crowded square is a slower process than I would like, and I worry about blending in even though no one seems to send much direct attention my way. Everyone seems occupied enough with their own doings. A wooden banner reading *Harra's Cloth & Leatherworks* hangs off the edge of a large tent, which shields several walkers working on stitchwork from the sky's random oppressive rays. A larger-set man, bearded and looking amply capable of felling trees and other harsh work, sits at the front finishing up what looks like a fix on a woman's brimmed sun hat.

"Here ya go. Good as new." He offers a smile, and the lady leaves after a quick thanks. "Needing something?" the bearded man asks, looking expectantly my way.

"I was searching for gloves. Harra's was suggested to me."

"Well, Harra's my name, and I'll gladly help ya." He stands, walks away some paces, and kneels down, grabbing a bin before heading back to the tent's front. He lays out a few pairs, some cloth, and some leather. "Let's see your hands so I know what sizes we need to be trying."

I bring forth my hands, palms up, and then rotate one hand while I retreat the other with my scar back into safekeeping.

"Ah, sure, sure . . . Probably try this size here first." He digs within the bin again. "You thinking a nice fitted leather or a cloth gardening glove?"

"Hmm, probably fitted leather. But sir, I have nothing to pay with right now except for my time. Is there some work you need done that I could help with in exchange for the gloves?"

He stays quiet while fishing around in the bin. "Ah, here's that blasted pair. Here, try these on. I got a feeling these were made just for ya."

The gloves are acorn in color, soft on the inside with polished exterior. They are a bit of a chore to get on, but damn do they fit and feel good after.

"Ha! What'd I tell ya? Perfect!"

I'm feeling a bit embarrassed now, as I really have no way of paying for, well, anything at the moment. And I've already got the fucking gloves on. The situation feels awkward, and I don't know what to say. "I had no idea such a fitted pair could feel so comfortable. This is some fine work, Harra. Is there some work I can do to pay these off?"

"That's not how it works here in the fields, son." Harra shakes his head, friendly in manner though. "Those of us that want to share our skills and contribute do so simply to help make this place even more amazing and plentiful than it already is. There's no quid pro quo here. Everyone gives out of friendship and care for another. You're new here. That's plain as day, but it's nothing to be embarrassed about. Things will get easier. Promise. That kerchief looks like shit, by the way." He points, then hurries about underneath the table. "Here, almost the same pattern but not tattered to high hell. Come on now, take it. It's yours, son."

Even though I'm told there's nothing to be embarrassed about, I still am. Can't shake it. Hell, I think I felt less embarrassed my first days in the Lowest, though I suppose shock took the place of any embarrassment that may have been.

"Really appreciate it, Harra. The gloves and all." I give a nod of gratitude and depart, making my way back the way I came, part of me hoping to see Gemma still playing near the edge of the asphodel field.

The bouncy spirit is not there though, either off with her "mum" or frolicking another area of the village spreading her charm, I'm sure. I escape the embarrassment of the unfamiliar village and walkers. The touch of flower petals across my palms is muted now, though their softness is still felt through the thin leather. The white flowers give way to familiar tall golden strands, which hug around me, hiding me. I become alone again and feel far, far away. Which right now, is comfort.

The night comes and brings with it new things. It's easy enough trampling down a small circle of the golden wheat to rest and bed in. And the distant sounds of the bustling village die with the bright hues of the grand sky.

As I lie on my back facing the blackness of the night hours, I find myself worried. Though I find myself enthralled too with the new sighting in the sky. The empty blackness becomes inter-rupted by a rising moon. Its traverse of the sky is slow and serves me well as a visual focus as I bury myself in the deep thoughts that barrage me this night.

There are no visual craters or abrupt disturbances on the moon like the one from the living world. Instead, the surface of this celestial body appears to have a grainy texture. I have no idea how far away it is or even if it exists at all on a physical level. *Does the End Realm have space?* Could the two blazing stars of the day be fictional as well? Just further examples of aspects of this world and its existence that are unknown to me. Though Tartarus had no skies like this one now. Definitely no stars or moons. *Hmm, I wonder if the arch-sorceress created the skies of this place. Perhaps everything above is but a mere painting, moving art—to give the field inhabitants a day and night cycle, and hey, while we are creating, why not make it as dreamy and captivating as possible?* My hand extends, reaching out to the painted moon, wishing I could know for certain of its origin, and hell, if it *is* a real celestial body, wishing I could visit and look to the fields, to Tartarus, to this realm, from that vast distance.

I withdraw my hand, and it rests on my chest. My eyes fix on the gray glow.

My feelings of worry that have been lingering since the lengthy descent from the High Sanctum are now more identifi-able. I think since I've been so distracted with entering the fields and headstrong and focused on seeking out how to hurriedly continue my journey, the sense of worry and panic remained but a cloud in the background of my mind that I couldn't clear because I was trying to bull-rush through to my next step. Lying here tonight though, I realize my worry is for Nahla—more precisely, the location I was told of during the truth ritual.

Nahla . . . in a hospital? I'm trying to not jump to conclusions and assume the worst, but it's becoming hard to not spiral into those thoughts. I can't shake the fear around this or the many questions and possibilities plaguing my mind. Such questions being: Is she in the hospital because she is gravely hurt or ill? Or is she in the hospital simply visiting someone else? I want to tell myself that it is likely for something very simple and not dire, but my fear is for the worst. The thought of her being in the hospital due to something of great significance is upsetting to say the least and brings weights of anxiety over me, along with the desire to want to be there with and for her in such a situation.

More and more, it becomes seeded in me that fear of disappointing and letting down those who are both important to me and who think they can depend on me is a strong part of who I am—and likely *was*. This all further solidifies that I always want to be a man of my word when it comes to my closest loved ones, and though this anxiety does not feel good, it does feel good to further know myself and understand who this Jaesyk person really is.

I do what I can to best clear my mind and focus my thoughts elsewhere. It is not productive to worry about such things—things I have no control over. And the feeling of guilt and shame of not being there with her (if she is in fact in a dire state) is not something I should ruminate on. That's not a smart way to utilize my mental energy because we are, well, worlds apart. If I want to get back and be there for her, I need to focus on spending my energy on the problems at hand, the road ahead. Not worrying about happenings or possibilities currently out of my reach.

After focusing on my breathing to settle myself, I force myself to make a plan of action. This is to be my first and last night in this field. When morning comes, I will take the short travel back to the village and take a stab at inquiring with some locals for any possible clues or guidance as to where I could go from here or who I could seek out to get myself closer to finding Hades or other possible ways back to the living world. Though I have a sneaking suspicion such questions may only get me odd stares and bewilderment. If I am met with nothing fruitful, then I'll choose a damn direction (albeit away from Tartarus) and travel by foot until I meet my next opportunity. For however long it takes.

With this settled and a plan at hand, I let the moon fade behind my curtains and welcome my own night sky. Hoping to dream of a time and space that feels like home.

CHAPTER TWELVE

Visitation

With the cadence of his large feathered wings and the fierce sound of the air assailing his ears at their current speed, Michael could not hear Chronos yelling to him but could easily see as he pointed down toward the golden field just ahead and to the west. Chronos's vision far surpassed that of Michael's, his insect eyes giving him the ability to see in different wavelengths as well as having greater depth of vision, so the archangel became used to this part of their friendship. Michael set the pace, and Chronos gave direction.

Since leaving Tartarus, the duo had set off at Michael's top rate of speed, and the two had not stopped since. They had already missed their opportunity to evaluate the time rift while this walker was in the Lowest, and they did not want to reach the High Sanctum just to end up giving chase again because the walker they sought had already departed.

Michael initially felt relief that they were finally making a stop as he had now been hours past the point of exhaustion. He could fly far distances without stopping, but he still had his physical limits. The time warlock was very lightweight, but at the vast distance they had already traveled, even that became an exponential burden.

As they continued the descent to where Chronos was directing them, Michael's relief became overridden with slight confusion. Yes, he needed to rest his wings, but their destination was close, within viewing distance even. The High Sanctum was a cloudy structure ahead on the horizon. Within the hour, they would be at its gate, and Michael could surely push through and close the distance without this stop. He didn't try to argue the point. Chronos must've been aware of something Michael wasn't.

The light of midmorning shone off the wheat and grasses below, causing their already golden colors to dance even more brilliantly. As their approach came nearer, Michael was able to guess why they were setting down. He could now see a figure and its casted shadow making its way through the golden field. And as their descent was not a slow one in the least, the figure, hearing their brisk approach, turned around so his pace was now backward, and he tensely watched the two boulder straight at him from above.

Michael's boots hit the ground hard and heavily as they met the narrow path of matted down wheat. Their forward inertia still being strong on landing meant Michael had to dig hard into the world below with his next few steps to halt the time warlock's and his own speed and travel. The force of the air being displaced around them from the archangel's wings and their aggressive fight against the speed caused the walker on the path in front of them to brace himself as the wall of wind smashed against his chest, nearly stealing the defensive posture he had assumed. Michael caught a glimpse of the walker's hair being forcefully whipped back from the wind as he, too, raised his hands, shielding his eyes from the assault.

Michael was not blind to the walker's disposition. He could see that this walker was standing as proudly and as unfazed as he was capable, though he was also aware of his fright and unease. Between Michael's stature, the unique physical attributes

Chronos was comprised of, and the duo's stark introduction, the archangel felt little surprise at the walker's current poise.

"Ah, all is well, friend." Chronos took steps forward and begged the walker with an open hand held up in a deescalating way. "We come with no ill will."

"No farther, please!" the walker called. And he, too, held up his hand but rather as a means to bring a halt. "I just woke and was on my way back into the near village. I want no trouble. I am sorry if this is your field. I meant no intrusion and will be on my way."

Michael could tell the walker just wanted to be on his way and to get away from any potential conflict or undesirable situation. Being as observant as he is, he took note of the gloves this walker wore as soon as he raised his hand. The garment seemed out of place here in the temperate fields. As did his place in these acres of wheat and his flighty mood . . . Was this walker, so out of place, the one they were in search of? Michael questioned.

The walker was taking his leave and began again on his matted down path.

Michael noticed Chronos anxiously rocking his head side to side in a sort of twitch and could hear his mandibles clicking fast. He was close to asking his time warlock if he would like him to intervene in the walker's progress, but just before he began, Chronos called again in plea.

"We truly mean no ill will!" Chronos voiced loud enough to get the walker's attention again, as he now had his back turned. "I know of your truth coins and your time spent with Karhon of the Rivers." With this, Chronos offered a short pause as the walker stalled even his very next step. "I know the Maw very well, actually. It was his aid that helped me understand where we may find you."

The walker turned then but stayed at his current distance while asking, "And why would Karhon want to help you do that?"

The archangel could hear the suspicion the walker had about the time warlock and the information that was just shared.

Chronos presented both hands open and out at hip level as he took a small step forward. "I understand your doubt of us. I am willing to answer any questions you may have. I just ask that we are given a chance to explain our purpose for traveling all this way in search of you. I believe we can both help each other, you and I."

"What is your name, and what is your real purpose here?" the walker asked in skeptical return, seeming to have been caught with some intrigue.

Chronos brought a hand to his shallow chest. "My name is Chronos," he said as his mandibles clicked, then pointed to the archangel, "and this is Michael. I am a time warlock. I record and calculate all time here in the End Realm. That is my post in this realm and also why I am here. It may not make sense to you in this moment in time, but I am here only for information."

"I've seen his kind before." The walker nods his head up, signaling aim at Michael. "And the interaction was not a pleasant one. And you . . . well, I've never seen and don't know of your kind, but you don't look all that inviting either."

The walker spoke with a sharp tongue but did not raise his voice or seem angry. Michael believed he was simply standing his ground as best he could while keeping his guard up. He found himself admiring this walker's intelligent reservation.

"An archangel, really?" Chronos asked, a little stunned. "Let me ask, when have you encountered another?" Chronos requested with vast curiosity.

"I had an unfortunate incident with the dark angel Rahkni while in the Lowest."

"Ah, yes. I see." The time sorcerer nodded. "The dark angel you speak of does bear a striking resemblance to my friend here. Both Michael and Rahkni are in fact angels, though I assure you, Michael does not, nor will he take commands from Alastor of Chains. And that likely is the reason your interaction with Rahkni was so unfortunate."

"You know of Rahkni too?" asked the walker.

"I am a time warlock, a recorder and computer of time, a library or database, if you will. I know of everyone and everything in the End Realm."

"Do you consider yourself a friend of Rahkni's?" the walker interrogated with a taste of possible judgment.

The time warlock paused for a moment before replying. "Rahkni is neither a friend nor foe of mine. I believe with that question you mean to further calculate your safety amongst Michael and me. As an officer, Rahkni's post is to follow the warden's command. With all the information I possess, I would say to you that although I recognize your unpleasant time with Rahkni, I assure you his soul is not as dark as his coat of feathers."

Chronos decided to quickly add, "Michael is also an archangel, which Rahkni is not—a title Hades only brands the most powerful and most loyal of angels with." Chronos turned his head a bit toward Michael. "He is here for my protection. If you haven't guessed, this shelled body of mine is fragile, and I am but a time warlock, not a warrior. My friend here would only turn on you if you were to attempt to harm me. That, I give you my word on."

Michael felt the air of unease lift a bit between the three of them. Even though the walker spoke sharply and at times processed things in silence rather than adding to the conversation, he could see the walker balanced a looser posture now, which Michael felt was a promising sign. His time warlock was succeeding in hiding it very well at the moment, but he knew of the distress, pain, and trepidation Chronos was going through as he stood in that field. It was the same distress he'd felt and battled since the time rift had been birthed, since this walker had entered the End Realm and his two truth coins rang on the solid stone under the Deliverance Gates.

As Chronos's post was to record and process time, Michael's post was to care for and protect the time warlock. Where Chronos felt distress when he couldn't process a *time*, Michael felt distress when his time warlock was feeling that distress. There was a link, a relationship between these two posts, Michael's and Chronos's. That was why their bond had grown so strong over their vast time together.

"All right, you say you can help me if I help you?"

Chronos clicked loud and slower than usual. "Well, that sounds transactional. I do not like that. I think it wiser for us to use the mentality of simply helping each other. Would you let us all sit and converse more? I am sure you have lots of questions, and I have much to explain. There is plenty of time for us to hear about how we could possibly aid you as well."

"I actually am in quite a hurry. I have much to accomplish and need to keep moving," the walker said with some anxious defeat in his voice.

Chronos clicked his mandibles in a loud and clunky yet precise fashion, much like the mathematical internal workings of sprockets and gears of a complex clock. He then placed both his index fingers between his large faceted eyes and then slowly brought his hands out in front of him while making sure his fingers remained together in that specific configuration. A small dark purple bubble whose surface wobbled as if it were made of a liquid began to grow between the two index fingers as the time warlock began increasing the distance between his hands. The dreamy bubble reached about the size of the walker's chest, and then Chronos thrust it straight down at the ground. Hitting the ground, the bubble instantly exploded in size, quickly rushing through all three of their bodies and creating a big dark purple dome around them.

"Thankfully, I can create small time dilation instances, like you see here." Chronos pointed around them at his summoned dome.

The walker was in awe at what had just happened. "What . . . the fuck is this?" he questioned ecstatically while looking up and around.

"While we are in this dilation, our time will move increasingly fast relative to those outside. While in here, we can continue our journey of helping each other, and you, my friend, won't have to feel so rushed."

"And if I desire to escape?" the walker questioned reluctantly while taking a glance over his shoulder at the edge of the dilation bubble.

"You are able to travel through the dome you see with no issue. The visible dark shell you see around us holds no physical value."

"All right. I am willing to stay and talk more. For now, I request you two still keep some distance from me. That is my only condition."

Michael saw the time warlock give the walker a cordial bow as he agreed to the walker's wish before sitting down and getting more comfortable in the field of wheat and grass. The archangel felt hopeful that his time warlock would soon be relieved of the duress caused by the rift that he was now working to close.

✪ ✪

Sidus was inspecting the towering cathedral doors at the entrance of the High Sanctum, looking in hopes of finding the evidence she so sought.

"Sidus, my dearest companion." Lunacrye stalled for a moment in bewilderment. "What in Hades's name are you up to?" The arch-sorceress was at a loss as to why her companion of so many years was motionlessly staring at the tall oaken doors that served as the High Sanctum's main entrance.

Sidus turned and raised her elevation to be at a more comfortable level with Lunacrye. "Scanning for fingerprints of the

133

human. I assume he took his departure since I cannot see his whereabouts but have not been able to locate you to verify."

"Oh, dearest. The door bears no fingerprints of Jaesyk. I opened the doors for him. I could sense a part of him wanting to stay, so I ushered him out as fast I could."

Sidus then harshly interrupted her: "I felt him a friend! Knowledge of his departure would have been of value to me!"

Lunacrye paused for a moment to give space in case Sidus was not done in her abrupt sharing of emotion. "I do apologize, Sidus," Lunacrye said with a soft breath of surrender. "I was unaware of any such connection you and our visitor had. I regret not knowing this."

Sidus's inner orbs swung low to one side, as if now she herself were feeling some regret. "No, Luna," Sidus offered. "You make an honest point. I never divulged any information about the fun and spirited time the human and I shared. I, too, apologize for being a bit of a crazy bitch just now."

The arch-sorceress let out a fast and short laugh—one greatly laced with surprise. "Uh . . ." Lunacrye caught herself in a chuckle again. "W-What was that?" She was in complete disbelief, to the point that she was fumbling on her words and wore an expression that Sidus had never really seen her wear before.

"Oh! Yes!" Sidus exclaimed. "That damned human taught me some new ways to use expletives, and I was so intrigued that I decided to research more of these 'swear words' as they are so called. I am simply broadening my linguistic databases. It is so much fun, Luna!"

"Oh, I see." Lunacrye nodded while attempting to hide her smirk.

"Yup! I think we could all benefit from a few cuss words here and there, Luna. You should try it for yourself sometime!"

With this, the crystalline sphere started her departure. And the arch-sorceress stood in her still air for a long while, wrapping her mind around and admiring the emotional complexities of one of her greatest of companions.

"Oh, my dear Sidus," Lunacrye said softly with a sigh and for only herself to hear as she was now in solitude at the tall oaken doors. "I am confident we will both have the pleasure of seeing that human again."

✦ ✦

Seeing Chronos and the walker sitting silently in the tall wheat grass brought Michael a vast ease. He felt comfort in knowing his time warlock was in the process of closing the missing gaps of information associated with this walker, who they now knew as Jaesyk. Michael's eyes went from the warlock's emerald shelled hands to the fresh morning skies of Asphodel and back again. The pair were holding hands as they sat in the field, and the walker seemed mostly intent on observing Chronos during the exchange, drifting his vision every so often to the same skies and to Michael as well. The archangel could tell the walker still had reservations about the two, but they seemed to have pushed past enough distrust to at least get started on closing the rift.

Michael caught himself thinking of the walker's shared story thus far and couldn't help but feel at odds with what this "Jaesyk" was attempting to accomplish. He also had suspicions that the walker was being carefully covert in how much of his story and direction he was sharing. Michael could not fully grasp the walker's desire to return to the living world. Nor could he fully understand what led the walker to believe such a feat was even possible. He could, however, understand the strong force and will that was driving the walker. Of course the archangel could understand the morality of staying true to oaths. After all, he had a driving force much the same within the oath he'd made to his time warlock and to Hades as one of the angels proud enough to boast the archangel title.

Memory and information exchanges varied in time. Some took minutes or less, like the last exchange Chronos had had with the Maw. Others, like previous times Michael had witnessed Chronos closing other time rifts, took an hour or even more. Being vigilant in keeping a close eye on the magical transaction between the two, Michael noticed no abrupt mandible clacking, head jerking, or any other signs of danger, and within the hour, the time warlock finally raised his head and gently let go of the walker's hands, retreating to his bony exoskeletal knees to aid himself in slowly standing after the length of time spent on the ground.

Michael gave all his attention then to Chronos. "Brethren, is the rift gone? Have we succeeded?" Michael questioned with both hopeful excitement and intrigue.

Michael could tell even with Chronos's inability to smile that a weight had been lifted from the warlock, making the next spoken words merely a confirmation.

"Ah, yes . . ." Chronos started, adding a couple clicks of his mandibles. "Yes, my friend. The time rift has been sealed. That does not mean, however, that there are no questions left unanswered." Chronos walked a few paces before stating that he must sit down, both to contemplate and regain some energy spent in the magical exchange.

Michael felt somewhat puzzled and knelt down next to the two. "How would the rift be closed, gone . . . and yet there still be questions left unanswered?"

Michael could hear Chronos clicking to himself as the time warlock held his hands in front of his chest and strummed his shelled fingers together. After more clicks and some pause, Chronos looked up to him.

"Friend, it is closed. Certainly closed! You see though, that simply means I have collected all the data there is to collect. And yes, typically after gathering all the information there could possibly be to record—well, there are no questions and therefore no information left to gain."

Still feeling confused, Michael attempted again to clear his ignorance. "But in this case, you're saying there is?" Michael held an open hand out, showing his puzzled nature. "If the time rift has been sealed, yet there are still questions that could be answered, does that mean that—"

"There are no answers," Chronos finished for him. "It means for whatever reason, the universe either does not have the answers or the universe has made it far enough out of our reach." Chronos clicked more. "Even *my* reach." And the time warlock bobbed his head in acknowledgment and resignation.

"Well . . ." Michael looked to the walker and then back to Chronos. "What is yet missing? What do we still not know? And most importantly to me, is the rift fully closed? Are you still plagued with any void—the feeling of something missing that you must find?"

"No, no, my friend." And Michael felt Chronos rest his hand on his left shoulder. "The weight of the time rift has fully been lifted from me. I have—*we* have succeeded, Michael." Chronos bowed his head slightly, then while he grasped his protector's shoulder tighter, he brought his brow in closer to Michael, almost in a way to show a certain intimacy toward the archangel. Looking to the walker, Chronos added, "Jaesyk has shown me much, and the three of us have much information, many possibilities, and yes . . . questions to discuss."

The walker, warlock, and archangel spent more time within the dilation bubble discussing how they may aid the walker in return for his willingness to comply with what Chronos needed. After which, they parted ways, Chronos and Michael walking at each other's side through the golden wheat away from the walker, opposite the nearest village.

Michael could tell something was amiss and had since the end of the exchange. He knew what Chronos had said about not getting certain answers was likely a falsity—one he guessed was to keep something from the walker. He looked down to Chronos, who kept his pace through the field.

"Chronos, there's something you're not telling me. I can see it in your eyes. This isn't adding up."

Some clicks broke the silent pause that followed the archangel's inquiry. "I didn't want to say it near the soulless . . . I saw something during the closing that I admittedly did not divulge. I saw a new age, a new dawn, a new dusk. He may be the very one the Devil-God has been rumored to be awaiting . . ."

Michael raised his brow, then: "Awaiting? For the purpose of?"

Chronos stopped in his tracks, looked to his companion—a look that told Michael he knew exactly of what he spoke.

"Then why not tell the walker? Knowing may aid him, drive him farther."

"If it is so, we mustn't interfere in any manner. His path needs be his own."

"I see," said Michael. "And what of his memories? Surely we've seen that exact happening before. Surely even the Maw has seen and understood such instances. Why choose to keep the truth from him?"

"Yes, friend." Chronos nodded his approval. "It is what you assume. His memories didn't fall with him. They are stuck on the living plane, much like we have seen before. And yes, Karhon has absolutely seen these occurrences, but you see . . . Karhon's way of managing his traumas is to forget—disassociate—as much as he possibly can while still keeping enough memory and thought to stay loyal to his post. The walker likely didn't get the truth regarding his amnesia from Karhon, because in Karhon's mind, he has never seen such an event before."

The time warlock took a moment, then started through the fields again. His protector took a solemn moment with his head hung, eyes blank on the golden strands, again thinking of the

Maw and how the more he came to know of him, the more he both respected and pitied the grimly cloaked son of Chronos.

CHAPTER THIRTEEN

Destination

N orth is my direction and Hermes Overlook my destination. The insect-like humanoid known as Chronos
and I discussed much the previous day. And although
I can't say I am taking his sound advice, I can say that I now
have a better grasp on my place here in the afterlife, even if that
means certain questions still having no found answer.

Chronos has the power to find, catalogue, and remember all
the happenings in the End Realm. He explained to me this means
having record of each and every soul (and soulless) inhabiting
this plane of existence, as well as how their life ended and what
living world they are from. Even small bits of information such
as the words they've spoken each and every day while in this
afterlife, down to literally knowing each and every footstep the
soul has taken—down to an exact location and time. I quickly
saw the immense power of Chronos, and it's easy now to see
him as a walking library. A perfect library, one with no missing
books or articles, one where no one can check out (and possibly
lose or damage) any of the books, one that is strong of will and
protected—one under guard and key, if you will.

After our time melding and closing the time rift my appearance here in the End Realm caused, I took advantage of the

situation as best I could, asking as many questions as time would allow, which turned out to be fairly vast. The time dilation bubble that Chronos conjured was no joke. I felt as though the three of us had spent half a day cycle together, yet upon walking out of the dilation's radius, I could see the morning light had barely changed at all. As if a mere twenty minutes or less had passed.

I am extremely grateful for our time together. I learned much and feel so much sounder and more grounded, so much more acceptance in not knowing certain things about myself, including how I got here. Because really, what I learned most was that there are no answers for some questions. Even after closing the time rift, Chronos still did not know certain pieces of information. And if Chronos—an immensely powerful time warlock—could not see and gain certain answers, then I surely have no place else to look. Except for maybe Hades, of course. I heard from Chronos that knowing such things simply is not possible, and although circumstances such as these are extremely rare and outside the norm, it is what it is, and that means there just currently is not a way for me to learn such things.

Chronos said he could not see how my life ended while I was in the living world and also that he could not tell why I was soulless or why I was gifted with two truth coins upon my arrival here. The time warlock also shared that he would not have known my name even after our melding and closing of the rift if it were not for him gaining access and being able to see the happenings between Lunacrye and me. He seemed fairly taken aback by this—that Lunacrye could see a piece of information about me that he, prior to our melding, could not. And the only reason he could see that spark of information now was due to our melding and him closing the rift.

I had several questions in regard to the time rift as well. But Chronos cleared it up fairly well, even though I still cannot grasp the reason for the rift's creation (must just be beyond my comprehension). Apparently, Chronos knew two coins had struck down near the Deliverance Gates, but that was all he could see. He could not see the coins' owner; he could not see what type of coins they were; he basically had no information about this new walker that had entered the afterlife. And it was quickly clear to me how abnormal that was.

As far as I know, a time rift is this vacant hole or hundreds of pages in a book that are blank, and Chronos can feel when such an instance occurs. He somehow has this innate ability to feel if there are blank pages in the vast library that is his to keep. It also was apparent how blank pages such as these are not a comfortable feeling to manage for Chronos. Not much was explained on this, but the archangel Michael seemed very concerned with the time warlock's discomfort—at one point asking if Chronos was still "plagued" by the recently closed rift, as if it were previously a source of anguish. The relationship they share caught me as unique and hard for me to grasp. In their explanation of their bond, I got the impression it was appointed, as if they did not choose each other but were appointed to one another at some point in time. Though I could also tell the intimacy of their connection is vastly deep and complex, making me cast my initial assumption of their relationship being "appointed" aside.

Our time together did prove mutually beneficial. Although the archangel stated he could not help in getting me across any vast distance because he needed to remain at Chronos's side, he did share some information, which is now my next (and only) lead in getting the fuck out of here. After the rift was closed and the conversation around that event concluded, I began explaining why I was seeking the Fields of Asphodel and the High Sanctum. I didn't get far in my story, however, as Chronos raised his emerald-green hand and cordially reminded me that he now knew of my past footfalls and time here in the End Realm. This struck me as unnerving at first, being reminded of this. It sank a little deeper than before when it had simply been explained to me in a broad sense. Now though, it was directed at *me*, and at first at least, a cloud of intrusion gloomed overhead.

After that, I truly understood just how precise this library of Chronos's was, and yes—*intrusive*. Even the conversations with Lunacrye are now in the books of his mind, and though this saved me time by not needing to explain my story and my current pursuits, it sure did bring on a sudden rush of vulnerability and nakedness. It doesn't matter how much I trust this warlock or not, my armor is down, and I am now a mere blip of pages in the halls of endless books. So rather than continuing to divulge my story and ongoing intentions, I decided to go straight to getting myself further on my path.

I asked about seeking an audience with Hades and was first met with blank stares, much like how I'd figured the local souls of the fields would react. Witnessing the time warlock and archangel offer such a reaction only confirmed how out of reach my hopes for a meeting truly are. I was told by Chronos that Hades is unreachable by even the Originals at times. The only times he knew of common souls being visited by Hades was on the Island of Eternal Truth (apparently a region unequivocally inaccessible to me). Michael chimed in on this, adding that Hermes—an Original who serves the Devil-God as messenger—is said to be the one who interacts with him most out of all in the realm.

I was eager to inquire more about this Hermes and learned that he spends most of his time traveling great distances throughout the realm, delivering messages and information to Hades, as well as the other Originals. He serves as the carrier of the powerful, delivering messages to and from all of the realms' leaders, walkers, and other inhabitants if the mission calls for it. This makes communication between the Originals and the Devil-God practical within their schedules. Practical mostly thanks to the astronomical speed at which the messenger can travel. From what Chronos said, Hermes has the ability to move so fast that most souls cannot see him when he's traveling at his fastest of speeds, most not having eyes capable of working at a high enough refresh frequency to register his presence. I'm keen on finding this messenger of the realm, and turns out, the time warlock and archangel showed no qualms about indulging me with what they knew of his whereabouts.

Hermes Overlook is a jutting mass of stone-scape that harbors lush moss, lichen, and a myriad of plant life—the most notable being the low and twisting juniper trees brought to attention by Chronos, who seemed to have an affinity for the trees, for when he spoke of them, his mantis-like mandibles clicked and clacked more excitably.

The distance to the overlook was explained to be extensive and not without its dangers. Two ways were given to me. One is to take a three-week journey west, reaching the far west end of the Fields of Asphodel, and then continue north-northeast, eventually passing through a centaur-inhabited region known as the Shallow Wood. Upon reaching the edge of the Shallow Wood, the overlook would then be visible far on the northern horizon. From there, it is an easy brisk trek through a flatter desert region—easy but not necessarily short by any means. In total, this would amount to approximately eight full weeks to get to the bottom of Hermes Overlook and then still the climb to its summit, where the messenger is said to call home. This way of travel was denoted by both Chronos and Michael as the *immeasurably* safer route, which bypassed the Tarr Mire.

My other choice is to head directly north from where I currently am in the fields. Going this way, I would still eventually reach the same flat desert-like region, but not without having to first successfully traverse—and survive—this Tarr Mire region, a place I was, unfortunately, adamantly advised to never step foot in. The Tarr Mire is a vast marsh region that spreads wider than the Shallow Wood and the desert region combined yet is still the much shorter and more direct path to Hermes Overlook. Michael urged me to travel the longer westerly route around the mire to avoid the many inexorable and ruthless species that thrive in the vile murky waters that span the entirety of the place, while Chronos expressed his concern about a much more baleful possibility.

The time warlock seized the air with his warning, trying to speak the true gravity of my desire to take that very route—the shortest, fastest, and most direct of ways. He never raised his voice or became violent, yet witnessing the direness in his voice and gestures was impossible to miss. Hihliah, known also as the riasce fairy or fairy demon, is an entity they said never leaves the Tarr Mire. She is a collector of flesh and souls from discarded prey items the other ruthless species of the mire have killed or playfully tortured—just to then be left alone to attempt their last meek chance at escaping the mucky lands. Chronos also labeled her in his urgent rambling as the Devourer, for she feeds on (or devours) wishes and regurgitates bad omens in their places.

So many fucking names just for one . . . *thing*? It would make me laugh if it wasn't for the tone and sincerity I was told in.

This fairy demon, Hihliah, really does sound fucking scary, and the immense warning Chronos gave in regards to entering the Tarr Mire does have me questioning my internal drive to charge into whatever would get me to Hermes Overlook the fastest. I have already almost had my afterlife ended in the pierce chamber, not to mention the physical pain and torture involved in that ordeal was nothing to shake a stick at. Those sensations of pain are not something I want to chase, yet I still have this internal conscience, this internal core of Jaesyk that makes me who I am, pressing and pressing at me. Almost forcing me to take whatever path would get me progress in the shortest possible measure of time.

I *have* to get where I want to be and where I feel I need to be. And right now, the next step toward that is Hermes Overlook. To take my try at seeing how the messenger can help me get closer to Hades or help in some other way in getting me back to the living world. I already have had other Originals prove helpful. If Karhon, Alastor, and Lunacrye were my first three gateways leading farther out of this hell, maybe Hermes will be the fourth.

Thanks were given from the two that descended on me from the sky, as well as hopes that I will find what I'm most looking for. In return, I offered a great deal of appreciation back, stating to them that I really had awoken with no real idea which direction or destination I would make my way toward after leaving that small spot in the fields. Thanks to them, I not only have a direction, but a destination. Two destinations, really. Hermes Overlook is one, yes, but the real desired destination is Hermes himself. I have a strong feeling this messenger is the next key. And so I set forth on a westerly bearing—though not for any longer than I had to. Only long enough for Chronos and Michael to see as they departed into the midmorning skies that I was proceeding on a bearing that would have me completely avoid the Tarr Mire.

As I looked over my shoulder moments later to gauge how far off they had gotten, I could no longer see their presence in the skies. A small piece of me felt a sense of loss then, reminiscent of that same feeling I had when I'd reached the last stair coming down from the High Sanctum, looking back up high on the stairs at the tall oaken doors and to where Lunacrye and Sidus were within. Admittedly, the sense of loss was stronger with those two, but I could still feel a small sense of bittersweet melancholy as I recognized the time warlock and archangel were gone. I took the time, standing in that space before moving on, to let that sense of loss and longing sit in my chest. It was not something I wished to cast aside and ignore. It was not like me to force myself to be stoic when I could instead sit with such feelings and grasp them for a moment. Grasp them with appreciation.

As I turned then to take my first step north, sending myself straight toward the Tarr Mire, the shortest path to the overlook,

I stopped dead in my next tracks as I stared blankly down at the wheat grasses that softly breezed across my elbows and flowed all the way to my feet. It hit me again—the precision and power of the librarian I had just met. I shook my head, at myself more than anything. That little facade I had put on with walking west as the two departed to hide from them my true intention of not heeding their advice to take the safer route around the mire was a waste. And completely transparent. It hit me that, of course, Chronos knew, and if not of my intentions, then he would for sure at least know of my next few steps. This upset me. I was false with them so they would not have any reason to put any energy into possibly worrying about me, and now . . . now if anything, I look like a liar. Which I do not enjoy. I gave a heavy sigh. And I said shallowly into the grasses, "Sorry." Then I began pressing on with my next steps, still keeping my gaze down into the wheat grasses for a short while as I continued on.

Then, and still even now, I am finding it difficult to get the regret of not being forthright with them out of my head. But I must let it go and not ruminate, for the Tarr Mire is ahead. I adjust my posture, stand straighter as I stride, bring my chin and eyes up more, and take as deep a breath I can, grasping enough acceptance to let it go and maybe even achieve some stoicism.

CHAPTER FOURTEEN

Stealer

G entle breezes, welcoming light rays spouted from skies above, cordial walkers, dry stepping ground, the feeling of safety . . . all have been replaced by an always brisk air, a shrouded cowl of looming cloud cast overhead, unnerving denizens, soggy wet mazes of ground surrounded by innumerable pools, the feeling of anxiety, the feeling of seclusion, the feeling that at any time, a chilling skeletal hand could lash out and grasp my very spine from within.

This is how drastically things have changed in my week of hasty travel. Each passing moment, I find myself speaking internally to myself in encouraging ways. Telling myself to keep moving, to ignore the distant screeches in the air, the thrashes of nearby water, the smells of death on the rolling fog. I tell myself to keep moving, to continue finding ways to sneak around the goblin-like creatures that I've noticed scavenging through the marsh waters, to push aside the intense fear (insects) and aloneness that comes to swallow and suffocate me. Regret is what deeply sits in my chest. Regret for not heeding the warnings and advice of the time warlock and archangel, for thinking it wise and myself strong enough to march through this forsaken fucking wasteland of ichor and putridness.

I want to sleep so bad, I think to myself, being that I haven't slept even a single minute the last two nights—my body, my mind, exhausted.

"Rhaaaahk . . . Rhakaaw . . . Rhaaaaahk." The now familiar but still chilling screech from some sort of winged inhabitant of the mire speaks out from high above the cloud cover.

Exhaustion is so set in that after my head swings up toward the high-pitched saurian-esque call, I realize the delay with which it took me to do so. *How physically and mentally done I am.* I shake my head in defeat. *To the point that I'm slugging along even in my reactions to potential dangers. I'm so fucked. I need rest, but there's nowhere dry in this shithole.*

The skies wield no visual of the creature. I have yet to catch a glimpse of one or *it* for that matter; I actually have no evidence against it being the same winged screecher that's possibly been following me since entering this seemingly endless bog. It is by far the loudest and most abrupt distraction here thus far. Only thing louder is the mass chorus of amphibious denizens during the darker hours.

Each new step is dauntingly the same. I lift my right foot from the suction of muck a foot below the water's surface. I gave up breaking the water's surface a day ago already, so I proceed to slog my foot and ankle through the dark fetid ichor-like water and let my weight fall with the step ahead, feeling it hit the initial resistance of the muck at the bottom and then slowly keep sinking until I find what's left of my decreasing strength to pull my left foot from the muck, mirroring the previous step. A rinse and repeat cycle this is. Although *rinse* is a word that almost brings a chuckle to me, as there is no rinsing the residue of this bog water off without a much cleaner source.

The smell of the Tarr Mire assaults my nose with every step. Every time I free my feet from the mucky sediment, an invisible plume of fetid and rotting decay wafts to hit my nose. I know the smell is mostly fetid vegetation, as the mire is dense with grasses, tall cattail-like reeds, and thick volumes of mosses throughout the mire's entirety. But there is something else too—an almost sour and warm stench that laces the gasses stirred up by my footfalls. Something definitely other than vegetation, something denser, something that rings in my head as . . . meat.

This is a place of death and cruelness. The days have been mostly quiet, but the nights . . . things move at night. Things scream at night. I haven't seen much, but I have heard things die in the dark hours. This is no place for me. This seems like a place only for carnivorous souls that are not interested in spending their time in the End Realm as pacifists. If anything, this place makes me think of the living world I knew, where there was an ecosystem—a food chain. This mire is a place souls are ever entering and ever leaving, as if there's a cycle of start and end here unlike any other region of the afterlife I've seen. Maybe this cycle works this way so that the mire cannot spread. I do not know. But surely the End Realm would be nothing but a pure hell if these creatures and this landscape were ever growing and its borders ever expanding. I felt fear in Tartarus, but here . . . here, I feel terror.

The slow slalom of fog drifts at a calmer pace so far today, which makes the dense patches last longer, along with my then compromised vision. Fortunately, this also means that the pockets of clear air last longer too. There is little to no verticality thus far. Every so often, a lone tree or two breaks through the foggy marshlands. Even still though, no semblance of dry land comes with such trees. They somehow root deep and wide enough to stand strong in the boggy pools, and much different they are from those I witnessed along the river's edge while with Karhon. The scattered trees in the mire wear dense and lush foliage. Everything other than the dark water here is cast in greens and grays. Trees wear green leaves that fight gray masses of moss for the touch of the heavy atmosphere. They appear nearly suffocated by the drab mosses, which hang from branches sometimes from a dozen feet or more all the way down to get a touch of the putrid water, yet the moss climbs as well, to every height the trees make available.

It is hard to see much. The reeds are tall here, just under eye level except for certain rare instances where the water deepens some. But just ahead (thanks to a pocket of clearance within the fog), I see the reeds turn to a more open area, where reeds find themselves replaced by mounds of sphagnum and peat, which I've learned offer a small respite from trudging through the resistance of water. A thick lush tree looks to stand alone deeper into the clearing—backdropped by more fog in the distance. A small swash of fog swirls through for a moment as the high-pitched screech assaults again from above.

"Rhakaaw. Rhaaaaahk!"

The volume, *much* closer now, rings back and forth in my ears. My hands bolt up, attempting to cup away the borderline painful zinging that bounces around, buzzing and vibrating the internals of my ears. As I duck down to obscure myself as much as possible in the tall reeds still some ways back from the clearing, I finally see this screecher as it dives down through the blanket of clouds and into the clear air that is caught between the cloudy ceiling and the low ominous layer of rolling fog.

Its vocalizations are much larger than the beast's actual size. I was expecting something much larger than me, though as it cruises down into the clearing of sphagnum ahead, I guess its wingspan is as tall as I am, and its composition is much mangier and thinner than expected. The winged creature looks much like a vulture from the living world, except this screecher has two necks, and heads accompany each.

It stands on its stilt-like legs amongst the dense patches of moss while one head seems to be tilting and pointing in different directions down into the water's edge, as if searching for a hunting opportunity. The other much calmer head stands nearly straight except to swivel slowly side to side, keeping an eye out for potential dangers, I presume. The screecher does this in silence for several moments, giving me some time to take in more details. It's skinny and malnourished (I think). This could be the normal aesthetic for this species. I guess I don't know for sure, but it doesn't appear healthy. It very much so resembles a vulture, though its necks are both much longer than the winged scavengers I know of, and this creature does not seem to be looking for an already dead meal. Everything about its posture and presence gives the impression that it's an ambush predator. Feathers and what looks like fur from this distance cover its body, the feathers being long and mostly found along the edge of the creature's wings and tail, while the deep iridescent black fur coats the rest of the gangly physique. As its odd dual necks and heads continue in their sentry and hunt, I realize why they look so out of place. They are protected by hard shiny reptilian-like scales rather than the softer feathers and fur. The screecher also has several old wound marks in places along both lengthy necks. The beaks are ivory in color and bold in size, while milky white eyes dot where one would expect.

After watching the screecher some, my nerves calm a bit, though I still don't dare to move in closer or make any movement or noise—not wanting to alert the creature of my presence, just in case. I keep my distance of roughly forty yards, staying inside the cover of the tall reeds that encompass the mossy clearing, my feet and ankles both now well rooted and sunk deeply into the mucky substrate under the mire water.

I'm getting impatient. I need to keep moving. I need to get the absolute *fuck* out of here, but the screecher still stands at the edge of the moss awaiting prey. The one head that stands tall and alert does not seem to take notice of me through the reeds, and I no longer fear this saurian bird. It really doesn't look as though it can be much of a threat to me. I should just give it a yell and make it bugger off, no? Or just start trudging through the clearing and hope that it promptly departs to the skies?

Yeah, fuck this. Time to move through.

Ggluumm. The shallow and quiet noise of my foot starting to be pulled from the muck gurgles beneath me. Just as I bring my eyes up again from the water at my feet, I quickly bring my planned movement to an instant and silent halt.

Oh shit! Don't fucking move, man . . . No more noise.

Something is ahead.

I try to control my breathing and stay as still and composed as possible. The blood in my veins pulses and *throbs* through my neck. I am afraid to even blink. Anxiety grows and grows—stronger and stronger—as I fear I'm not being still enough. It seems like my whole body is bouncing, making movement with every new surge of blood. Breathing is hard and as if I can't keep up with it. A mass swells in my throat. I try not to even swallow out of fear the action would somehow be seen. I feel like I'm suffocating, trying to make my breaths as shallow and quiet as possible.

Ahead, just past the screecher at the side of the lone tree, steps out a bony and raggedly sharp-featured goblin with wide slit-like eyes of milky color. The milky eyes appear to pierce even through the misty air. Its elongated pointed ears peek above and from behind its shallow head. The goblin stealthily stands still next to the tree, low to the mossy ground in a half crouch. It's looking right at me. It doesn't blink. Or is it staring down the screecher?

Several beads of sweat reach the peak of my brow, threatening to gain enough weight to fall farther and drip their salty way into my eye. Another tickles the very end of my nose, attempting to persuade me to make myself found by moving to swat away the nuisance.

Ages seem to pass, though certainly not even a minute has come and gone. The pale green-skinned goblin starts sneaking its way toward the screecher and me. Its movement looks much more fluid and poetic than the creature's physical form. Most of the creature's physicality reminds me of the imps Alastor of Chains magically brought forth from the main wall of Tartarus. Though this goblin's skin is more gray-green compared to the rusted reds of the imps, and the creature's milky eyes and lengthy ears bear further striking differences.

The lumpy mass of anxiety and panic in the back of my throat remains; however, the hollowness in my chest seems to calm some as the goblin's target becomes more clear as the screecher rather than me. The salty buildup of sweat at the end of my nose falls into the dark bile waters that house my submerged feet. The air here is so quiet that the drop of sweat meeting the surface is audible, causing the hollowness in my chest to quickly pulse in size for a moment. But the white-eyed goblin continues to stalk low and forward, not seeming to take notice of the fallen droplet inside the reed line. I remain as motionless and silent as I can, gazing intently on the two creatures in the clearing ahead. As the goblin closes the gap to the screecher, I notice that though they are clearly very different, they are also similar. The all-white milky eyes of the screecher match exactly the color and shade of the goblin's. And their thinned-out anatomy—almost as though both are starving—is quite impossible to miss.

Even with the screecher's one head standing tall and panning its view of the edge of the clearing, it somehow still hasn't taken notice of the encroaching goblin, now closing in within fifteen yards. The stalker moves with skill that injects fear in me, such a steady and silent ambush. One could be gaining ground on me from behind even right now. Or in the middle of the night when all the light is gone and my human eyes are complete trash.

The screecher shoots both heads up in an instant as something has finally been noticed. At the same time, the goblin lowers its stalking crouch even more. The two heads of the screecher both shoot their investigative gaze straight in the direction of the goblin but seem to be looking well above and over its pursuer. The goblin freezes in its low stance, the screecher now using both heads in unison, scanning to the right, toward my position in the reeds. It begins scanning then to the left, back over the top of the motionless stalker, and continues far enough left that it lifts one of its thin stilt legs to help bring its body the same direction—a sore mistake. The goblin lunges from its crouch, sailing through the air with speed before the screecher's leg has a chance to reach the sphagnum. Wretched bulbous knuckles and long thin mangled fingers stretch out, leading the attacker's way through the air.

The screecher dips its body low as it is so harshly startled, likely in an attempt to then push off from the sodden ground, but its attacker has skillfully gotten itself in a far too advantageous position for such a reaction to have any merit.

"RAAAH—" the creature's high-pitched primal cry of surprise is interrupted as one of its necks is chokingly ensnared in the mangled grasping off-green hands.

"Rugh—"

"gulh— ra—"

"aaagl—"

Screaming and pleading sounds are choked off and interrupted numerous times as the two do their dance of grotesque murder and escape.

Keeping myself still and quiet in the reeds becomes not nearly as important now that the air is imbued with slogging sounds of feet stomping the sodden peat in the clearing, the choked-off gargling screams of the screecher, and the rasping hard breaths of the murderous goblin scrambling to induce final death unto its prey.

The goblin wrenches at the neck it has a grasp of with violently sharp actions as the other head faces away toward its bounding direction of escape. The screecher hops away as much as it can in meek jumps, only to be violently shoved back to the ground each time as the goblin forces itself atop the bird as much as it can manage, slamming it to the boggy ground over and over again, every continued primal and desperate attempt to escape the clutches of the raging attacker failing.

The sound of several vertebrae cracking all in a single moment resonates from the dance of death ahead. The one neck being worked first is finally set free from the goblin's vise grip, and it falls limp and lifeless to the bird's side, now being dragged through the mossy peat while the screecher continues to bound, trying to get airborne. The bird pushes off again, bringing its broken neck and lifeless head into view through the reeds as it gains another short burst of altitude. With another loud rasping breath, the goblin tightens its grip on its prey and pushes forward again with a now exhausted lunge, crushing the screecher down into the sodden ground, predatory teeth from a wide and hurriedly expanding mouth give another, more carnal lunge.

"Rah-LK—"

A final sickening yelp cuts the fogged air like the coldest of knives. Wet slogging sounds come from the now quiet clearing, the goblin's razored teeth biting down harder and harder, and then after one last clamping bite that produces the sound of a once saturated sponge being wrung tightly one final time to ensure there's not another drop to produce, the entire mire falls soft and silent again as the goblin brings its head up. Blood rolling down its chin and its slit-like milky eyes scanning the surroundings quietly, it stands over its murderous victory. And with that silence comes again the waves of anxiety and lump blocking my throat as I realize I, too, need to become silent and unseen.

After a moment of scanning its surroundings to ensure it is alone and can feast in safety, the goblin reaches down and begins ravaging the screecher's corpse. I cannot see much of the screecher now that it has become a fallen victim, though the goblin seems to be working quickly on a specific part of its prize. The sounds of wet tissue being pulled apart and slurping sounds of gristle losing suction echo through the misty air. The sounds of the butchering run through my ears, and my hand comes to my mouth. I'm trying to hold back vomit. A hot splash of acid sears across the back of my throat. I swallow. Rank sourness hits my nose from the inside. I swallow hard once more, twice again, attempting to clear the taste and smell that I *know* I won't be free from anytime soon. I keep a tight grip over my mouth. Losing it right now would surely catch the goblin's attention.

Through the fog, the goblin takes a proud, more vertical stance. It lifts its hands, which cradle the milky eyes of the screecher. The goblin slowly, almost with awe, as if it were a precious gemstone, plucks one of the eyes from its cradled hand and holds it high above its head, staring at it while some of the light through the fog glistens across the milky white ball. The goblin seems to be unhealthily overtaken by its prize, as if it were something of great importance or addiction.

It carefully returns the one eye to the bowl of its other hand and begins chomping down into the cradle of eyeballs. Grotesque sounds of rupturing membranes, wet soupy tissue being slurped, and the goblin's razored toothy mouth mashing against itself comes to my ears, making me wince my eyes shut and shake my head back and forth in somber disgust. Milky fluid rolls through the goblin's fingers and drips down to the ground. The goblin raises its head, its own milky white eyes now bulbous and *wide* open. No longer are they thinly squinted and devilish in nature. The goblin's razor-filled mouth hangs open, slack, fluid from its meal oozing and rolling off its chin, its eyes now round and massive. It stands there staring in one direction, not giving a single blink.

"Rhakaaw! Rhaaaaahk!" Again, a familiar high-pitched screech rings out from the skies above and off in the distance, far past the clearing. The goblin snaps its blink-less gaze up toward the call, quickly deciding to leave the rest of the screecher carcass for its newly heard prey—in the opposite direction of me, thankfully. As the goblin disappears into the far fog of the clearing past the lone tree, I bring in a deep breath—a much-needed breath, one I needed to take several minutes ago but fought hard not to out of fear that even a normal-sized breath would be heard.

A lot runs through my mind. I have been in a constant state of fear and danger since entering the Tarr Mire, but the events that just unfolded have sent that fear even deeper. And why did the goblinoid leave the rest of the carcass untouched? Surely there is meat and edible parts of the screecher beyond its four eyes . . . Something happened when it bit into those eyes though. It almost looked as if it brought a euphoria to the goblin, a high of some sort. And even before it began ravenously consuming them, the goblin treated them with a deep reverence. Staring at them, inspecting them as if they were jewels. Every area of this realm I've seen thus far has had vast differences, but this place . . . This fucking mire is pure alien to me. And pure discomfort and fear.

Night comes again after I tread carefully and slowly onward, still with a north heading. Again, I am met with blackness and the chorus of thousands of what I can only guess are amphibious creatures of this swamp. And again too, the many soft white glowing orbs seen moving in and out throughout the tall reeds and cattail-like marsh plants. I guess it's purely luck that none of the glowing orbs get close enough for me to verify any identity, though I start to assume now—and fear—that they are the milky eyes of more of the mire's inhabitants. I fight sleep as it starts to come. I am exhausted and feel my body finally able to drift away into dreams but fight it with as much strength as I can. I no longer want to sleep, not here . . . not in this place. Not . . . in . . . this . . .

✹ ✹

The pale light from the skies above softly engulfs rolling mist as it slowly passes across my field of view. Grogginess wanes. *Fuck . . . I fell asleep.*

I choose not to move. Instead, I just lie here on my back looking up through the view of tall reeds leading up into the misty fogged sky. I am so fucking sick of this place. The peat I was sitting in during the night must have given under my weight, or the blackened swamp water rose in this area, as I am now lying on my back almost fully submerged. Only most of my face and chest are exposed to the chill damp air. Both ears are clogged full of the fetid water, giving the sound of my breathing an echo-y resonance. I feel dour and the somber desire for resignation.

"I wish I was out of this fucking hellhole," I meekly say aloud. "This fucking swam—" I halt, that last word sheared off as my eyes go wide, realizing I may have just made a wish. A wish in the Tarr Mire, where Hihliah the demon fairy and devourer of wishes reigns—what Chronos desperately warned me of.

"Hee-he." A small fiendish voice giggles balefully. "She's going to liiiike this little piece of riches!"

I bolt up, breaking away from the blackened water, and cast my wide eyes toward the voice coming from just at my feet. Right in my space stands a goblinoid, but not nearly the same as the type I saw devour the screecher's eyes. It stands short, only a couple feet tall, with pinkish gray skin, though not as clean and uniform as a human's. It dons simple but ragged old leather armor and a tattered leather satchel slung over and around its shoulder.

"Hee-he . . ." The goblin chuckles wryly again with a grin while it takes its gaze from me down to its own hand, where in an elegant well-practiced manner, it is rolling a coin across its knuckles.

Where it is rolling my other and last fucking truth coin across its knuckles . . .

CHAPTER FIFTEEN

Eater

With desperate haste, I bring myself up from the murky water and stand tall over the tiny goblinoid creature. "You give that *back*, right now!" I state with heavy and gritty weight, pointing sternly at my coin.

The creature is extremely small. Towering over it now with my stature brings me confidence that this goblin poses me little threat. However, the vulnerability of seeing my truth coin in another's possession has instantly hollowed out my chest—a frozen stone where my heart would be, exuding its chill in the dark barren cavern.

My coin is flicked into the air by the goblin's thumb. My vision sinks into it as it spins over and over in the misty atmosphere—creating the appearance of a small gold sphere levitating. With fast hands, the creature snatches one of the many leather pouches from its belt and opens it an arm's length under the sphere that is now being pushed down by the gravity of the realm. All I can do was watch, as these movements the goblin makes are so lightning fast. My vision targeted on the gold sphere ends abruptly with the image of the creature's tiny nimble hand clenching together in a fist as it cinches the leather pouch tightly closed, safely imprisoning the coin inside that I am mentally racing straight for.

"Ope!" the goblin lets out in a surprised manner as it looks up at me with widened eyes as though it was all a mistake. But it is clearly a snide sarcastic reaction, playing jest at me, a maniacal way of rubbing in my face that the theft was my own fault—a sleeping victim makes for an altogether easy heist.

Before springing forward and ripping this creature's head off its tiny body, I give it one last chance. "Give it . . . NOW!" I slam my words. Low and stern. Palm held out.

"Hee-he!" The creature giggles its same giggle again and bounces its hairless eyebrows as it smirks its thin wide lips. "Oh, I don't think it so," it says in its high and tightly raspy voice. "She will give me many, many eyes for this little rare piece of riches!" The goblin quickly snaps its chin to the side, giving me a fast sinister look out of the corner of the only eye now meeting my own, then bolts away in a mad dash through the tall reeds.

"NO!" I yelp out as I frantically slosh forward through the shallow waters.

I rush, bounding through the marsh reeds as fast I can, the shallow black water being aggressively displaced as my feet pound through with every quickened step. Fetid splashes launch up at such force that my face and mouth keep catching some of the displacement. Keeping up with the tiny creature is extremely difficult as it zigzags and weaves through the terrain with far more speed and dexterity than I am capable. The creature pops in and out of view through the reeds. I catch glimpses of its many pouches and main satchel jostling up and down as it darts through the marshland, enough for me to follow to some degree. But I can tell that the little fucker is getting away from me.

Breathing heavy, muscles fatiguing, and constantly bringing hands to my eyes to clear out the murky water being splashed into them makes the chase a losing battle. I realize I am not going to catch the creature, though I remain headstrong and keep my pace and pursuit as I best can, hoping that the terrain will eventually offer me an advantage or at least the possibility of seeing the damned thing enough to follow it to its home or to this "she" who would pay so handsomely for the coin.

The goblinoid's pace doesn't falter, though I still catch glimpses through the reeds every so often, and I happen to see a few things jostle free from its satchel slung around its shoulder. It either doesn't notice or it deems getting to its destination or even farther from me more important. The creature weaves through the reeds in a way I simply cannot, so I pound through the tall vegetation in direct lines; it is the only reason I am even remotely keeping trail on the bastard. *I'm going to wring that little fucker's neck and rip each of its fingers off one by one. That's my coin, damn it.*

Suddenly, my next step plunges into water that is several feet deeper. The deep hole trips me up, and I haphazardly lose balance, falling to my left hip, splashing water and swamp debris everywhere. I wince my eyes tight as the massive splash shotguns into them. I stumble and hurriedly manage to get to my feet again. I have to stop for a moment and clear my damn eyes, get a better view of my surroundings and this deep water hole that practically just ate me. It looks like I've happened into a small clearing, only about five yards in diameter. It is mostly water here, too deep for reeds to grow, so the tall reeds surround me on every side. I look down and quickly slough the rest of the water off my face using both hands. Just a foot from me is unmistakably an eyeball with a few nerve endings tailing off it floating in the freshly rippled water. I look around quickly, making sure nothing's rushing in after me, then back to the eye.

The white milky eye lies atop the water, matching the ebb and flow of the now softening ripples of the disturbed water hole. This must be one of the things that jostled free from the goblin's satchel. If it has any idea just how valuable that truth coin is, it likely won't be interested in bargaining, but I am not about to let that possibility pass me up, so I snatch up the rogue milky eye, find the creature's path on the other side of the deep hole, and continue my pursuit. Yesterday starts coming to mind, with the goblin and screecher. And how it seemed that goblin would have done anything to harvest the eyes of the two-headed bird. As I move onward, I find myself instinctively adopting a slower, more methodical, stealthier and cunning advance. This time, *I am* the goblin. This time, *I am* the hunter. And this time, that thief is my screecher.

I continue following the creature's trail through the reeds and swampy terrain. Time and exhaustion seem to stop. I feel as though I lose track of them, and the only thing of focus is the hunt, the stalk.

The goblinoid is no longer within a distance to be heard or seen, though its trail is fairly easy to track as it was in such a rush and didn't care to be delicate in its movement. Generally, it's been very difficult to traverse with any amount of speed in this forsaken place silently because of the rarely escapable water. I'm playing the long game now though. I know I can't outrun the sneaky little shit, so there's no reason to rush. My stealthy advance aids me in remaining mostly unheard, even to myself. I keep moving onward, taking care to stay on the creature's path, which it has barreled through with enough force to mash down the reeds in a narrow curving trail. I'm careful to move my feet forward through the now shin-deep waters instead of breaking the surface, and round my shoulders through the tall reeds so as not to disturb the loud stalks. This eventually proves fruitful. I finally come to a change in terrain as another sphagnum and peat-filled clearing comes to view ahead.

A few more slow and steady strides ahead, weaving my way fiendishly through the marsh, gives me some view through the still many reeds between me and the soggy peat clearing. Manipulating my view through the curtain by slowly reaching my head in different angles brings a view of what appears to be a hut of some sort, looking to be fashioned mostly of small tree limbs and the very reeds I find myself hidden within. Intrigue catches my now reptilian brain. I feel as though Jaesyk may have been left behind. I feel this place changing me. And I feel like the hatred and disdain I have for that thief has pushed me far enough away from my humanity that I am now at home in the Tarr Mire, hunting for not only my belonging . . . but a head.

A few more low roguish crawls forward bring me within mere inches of the reed line. And explosive volcanic ire rushes, my jaw tightens, and my teeth clamp down hard against each other. Warmth of the lava courses from my core out to my extremities, as I can now see *the thief.* Seventy yards out, near the opposite side of the clearing, the goblinoid paces farther away with its back to me, now merely walking, its previous agility and haste no longer needed as it continues forward. It holds its hand out, and a split second of morning light creaks through the foreboding overcast above, letting off an unmistakable quick shimmer of gold radiance from the tips of the thief's fingers.

The hand reaches toward another hand. With my vision so pinned on the goblin, I failed to fully grasp the plot ahead. The goblin is heading to meet a human—a beautiful female human. She stands not far from where the hut of reeds previously was; however, my eyes must be failing me . . . as clearly, it is now not a hut at all, but a finely built cabin home. One with a chimney billowing soft smoke into the overcast as far as the eye can see and a simple porch that runs along the front. There are no other notable features in the clearing other than a handful of narrow shoulder-height tree trunks that are far past dead, holding no branches or leaves.

The tiny thief approaches the woman, hand held up high, offering her the golden loot. The woman accepts the gift and speaks something into the goblin's ear; however, with the distance, the conversation is far too muted for me to pick out any of what is said. The woman reaches into her silken white dress,

165

bringing forth a small cloth pouch of her own. She places the coin inside. I become caught off guard. The predatory and ireful focus I had has waned instantly, bringing a bout of confusion and intrigue. The woman's white dress resembles the one Lunacrye wore, so much so that I shake my head and widen my eyes. The woman *definitely* is not the arch-sorceress; the crescent moon shape of her head and overall facial features are unmistakable. This woman appears to be human and of middle age. The dress though . . . it is enough to completely take me from the focused and animalistic passion I was entrenched in.

The woman kneels a bit and pats the goblin on its hairless head. Words continue to be shared softly amongst the two before the goblin bounces off and into the warm and homely cabin.

I start to think it will surely be easier to get my truth coin back now that I am dealing with a human—someone I can reason with and not some scheming creature of the fucking mire. But the woman takes a single step farther from her cabin and then stands still, hands held together at her navel. Restful, she slowly scans the entire edge of the reeds around her encircled clearing. The speed and way with which she so intently scans the reed line sends a cold breath across the back of my neck. The scene before me now feels ominous . . . and haunting. And that same lump that formed in my throat the day prior has now suddenly returned. I sink back a mere few inches into the reed line—enough to help me feel more unseen but not enough to catch the woman's eye or ear—although the sudden fearful anxiety that's now gaining control over me is screaming at me to not move, breath heavy, or even blink.

I reluctantly give myself permission to wince my eyes shut. To refresh them with the much-needed moisture and comfort of my eyelids. Rather than being met with the relief of finally blinking, I instead startle, engulfed with terror. My hand slaps the water—hard!—trying to catch myself after tripping in my sudden backpedal from the scene. In that one blink, my ears hear a split second of horrific screams. The high-pitched wail of a child or young woman. In that split second, my eyes see an old grotesque witch in the clearing ahead, surrounded by wooden pikes that skewer the flesh of bodies, holding them as tortured trophies. In that split second, my nose sears with the burning stench, the odor of warm decay . . . of rotting flesh.

Fumbling fast, I gain footing again and dart my eyes forward, looking up to the clearing through the reeds. The scene is again of a beautiful woman in white, paired fittingly with a visually inviting cabin.

The woman takes another—this time very direct—step forward. In my periphery, I plainly see the hard ripples of the water pulsating from me. My stumble and thrashing were most obvious, and so too is the direct stare the woman sends my way. I don't know if she can truly see me in the marsh's foliage, but our stares seem to pierce each other. The woman looks very fair; however, she does not feel fair or beautiful any longer. An ominous potency radiates heavily from the clearing. The reeds do nothing to shield me from this assault, this terror. As she stands motionless, folded hands still resting at her navel, a slowly widening grin creeps across her fair face—showing a grandiose smile, one that could normally be seen as pleasantly inviting but now feels deeply perverse.

"Ah, my dear . . ." The woman speaks in a voice that's softly young and reassuring. "It seems something has mistakenly been taken from you."

Another harsh wave of evil permeates through the reed line, rushing through the core of my torso like a crashing wave carrying the weight of a thousand oceans. It crushes my rib bones, causing me to gasp for a large breath in the fog-filled humid air.

"Oh, how the mist is so harsh on one's lungs out there." The woman speaks again in her soft voice, the awkward teeth-filled smile now a sympathetic slight frown. The woman continues to stay otherwise motionless, her beady eyes still piercing my direction. "The clearing here," she continues, "offers kinder air." She waves a hand out, gesturing her invitation to the clearing in which she stands before returning it to her navel.

Curiosity, as well as strong thought, pulls my attention to the milky white eye I still grip, though now tightly and in fear at my side. The strong pull hits with another wave. *Something is wrong with this here. This will show me . . .* Something is screaming at me that this will show me.

Without another thought, I jam the almost fist-sized eyeball against my mouth. I bite my teeth down, forceful and fast, then with the grip I have on the eye, tear it away from my clenched teeth. My mouth is shot full of cold oily fluid. Wetness drips down my chin and off the fingertips of the hand still holding the other half of the once whole milky globe. Before I can force a swallow, my brain buzzes hard. My pulse races through my teeth, *pounds* through my teeth. My eyes go wider than I ever thought possible, and my jaw falls slack, my mouth hinged open. I see horror and murder ahead of me—though too a euphoria and buzzing high courses through my veins and through my brain that I never knew possible. The high comes pounding at me so fast and strong that I go catatonic. In this euphoric buzzing bliss, I float and stand in horrific stupor.

The blinking flash I had was a flash of truth. Ahead of me, through the reeds and in the clearing, now stands a hunched witch, a gross ugly hag wearing nothing but rags and a belt full of sewn flesh pouches and flasks. Her face is riddled with scars from burns or acid. And her head shakes uncontrollably from side to side in minor convulsion as she stands under the now tinged red and far more darkened skies than before.

"Ahk!" the wretched hag scorns, lowering her gaze at me through the gnarled greasy hair that falls from her scalp. "You . . . you stupid *fucking* cunt of a human!" she spits venomously, saliva dribbling from her mouth.

She turns and starts jaggedly pacing her corpse-like body toward the nearest pike sticking out of the mossy sodden clearing. As she does, she brings her hands off her navel and holds out a sphere of smoky crystal quartz, which she must have been embracing this entire time. The sphere is held out and discarded as if it were trash, no longer useful, and let to fall and sink into the bed of peat.

"Now worse things must happen . . . to get you in here to barter with me," she spits as she approaches the nearest pike, the nearest horrifying scene. "Now, enter the glade, or this disgusting baby loses its other"—she grins wryly under her mess of hair—"leg."

My mouth is hinged open, still unable to move. Catatonic. The blood in my head rushes so fast that my teeth, eyes, and brain buzz hard in constant static. As the hag speaks in a harsh tongue, all I can do is watch as she drags her body over to that nearest pike—where there's a living, breathing, gasping and screaming one-legged baby. The infant's bare body is mostly covered in blood, but it looks to be either human or possibly dareen. It wails and wails, as though the pike clearly stabbed through its body and out the top of its head somehow has not ended its afterlife, but rather keeps it in a state of immense continued pain. It's somehow still alive and *feeling*—likely wishing constantly for a savior, for freedom from hell. I want nothing more than to look away from the pain in the clearing ahead, but my body is immovable from the fluid still dripping out my mouth covering my chin. My widened eyes see the entire clearing—numerous pikes, all trophied with gruesome displays of humanoid beings screaming and yelling in dire agony. There must have been some magic preventing this all from being truly seen and heard before. Something the narcotic in this eye fluid was able to dispel.

The hag grabs the infant's remaining leg. "Come," she sneers. "Come to me and your coin, or I'll rip this dreadful thing's limb and feed on it further."

I want to scream. Louder and more painfully than even the naked baby. For I do not want this, any of this . . . I want to save this poor soul. I want to run away from here. But neither I can do. I know that much. I can only feel the tears spill from the corners of my eyes as the cruelest of all things happens, my eyes stuck wide open as the horrific scene unfolds in front of me through the tall reeds.

My brain's overtaken with drug, with trauma, with horror. My eyes are still glued open by the euphoric buzz, but something about the visual ahead becomes a white-hot blur. A blur of disassociation, of traumatic distortion. I can feel the evil of that clearing still hitting my chest and permeating through the reeds and marsh grasses, and though I can physically still see the hag while she further destroys the body of the poor infant soul agonizingly skewered on the pike and all the morbidity within that space, it's like my brain only lets me see this white-hot ember-like blur.

I feel the wet torn-in-half eyeball roll out of my hand. The splash of water causes a blink, and my attention shoots down to the floating milky object atop the rippling dark marsh. The high still courses through my eyes, my teeth—hell, it's even buzzing in the bone structure that is my very skull. Though I am at least aware enough that even in the overwhelming euphoria, I moved my head down to see where the eye fell in the marsh. It takes all my strength and will, but I try to force my body to turn and can feel my body and vision turning where I tell it to go. Everything moves slow and buzzes with static, buzzes with confusion. But I keep forcing my will. However slow, I keep moving.

I hear scorning reverberate from the hell circle, and the constant wailing of wishes and pleas from the piked prisoners continues through the tinged-red air. I start to run. Everything looks to drift and drag in blurred motion; everything feels so very weighted. Splashes sink behind me like something or someone is on my heels—something giving chase—or is it the drug playing games? The caw of a bird cleaves the air from the bloodred storm above.

I want to run fast, but it all feels so slow. I run slow. But I keep running. However slow it is, I keep running that slow.

I keep running away, weighted . . . slow . . . but I run.

And I run.

And I run.

CHAPTER SIXTEEN

Despond

This . . . this is where Jaesyk gave up. He had lost all hope and began questioning the very path he had so strongly believed in and set forth for himself. So much so that as he took his first steps out of the Tarr Mire and into the desert region, he angrily clenched his ring of wedlock in his fist as hard he could and chucked it as far into the deadly swamp as his hatred and strength allowed. The act brought him great sorrow, but was the only way he felt he could accurately express the abyssal despair he was in.

Jaesyk's escape of the Tarr Mire was expeditious, even though to him, it felt as if he were unable to move his body with any true speed. The euphoric high caused by ingesting the eye fluid from any of the mire's inhabitants brings on massive perception changes. In most cases, this vitreous fluid drastically slows the perception of time and one's perception of their own speed and physical capabilities. After Jaesyk had come down from the vitreous high, he was quickly able to see how this fluid was an integral part of both life and death in the mire, as it alters what the recipient can see—sometimes seeing through false illusions, other times gaining the ability to see through the clouds and fog that otherwise plague one's vision in the vast wetland landscape. Creatures fight and kill for the fluid as a means of survival there, at times putting it above even their own health and nourishment. And more so, they even barter with the fluid as if it were a form of invaluable currency. In ways, the drug is the very heart of the Tarr Mire. And it made sense to him then—after escaping—that such a dangerous, faithless, sullen, and toxic place was run on such a vile substance.

He didn't just leave the mire behind. The Tarr Mire acted as a clear-cut line—the end of many things for Jaesyk. He left his ring behind. He left any ambition and will to return to his wife behind. And he had altogether left purpose behind, purpose of any kind, far back and long behind him. And he was not returning for any of it.

Jaesyk traversed the barren desert, which reminded him of the treacherous and jagged black stone landscape he had found himself in upon first entering the End Realm. He thought of the Deliverance Gates, how immense those solid doors themselves were, and how the sound of them slamming shut behind him echoed in his mind still as if it were a curse. A cursed reminder of the finality of those doors, a reminder of how tall and vast they were, a reminder of how dense and impenetrable they were, a reminder of something he had failed to see this entire time . . . that he was *shut in*. A cursed reminder that he was not meant to return to the other side.

And so he traversed the jagged desert of sharp obsidian, though it was not to continue as far north as the mountains where he would find Hermes Overlook, but to merely get enough distance from the Tarr Mire and the Devourer to feel assured he was out of reach of such horrors. He walked for what he could only estimate would be equal to two day cycles within Tartarus, as the skies here seemed to remain starless and dark—much like the never-ending hollow black of the skies over the river Karhon ferried. This region was much the same, albeit with far less trees and shrubbery, the absence of the river, and the jagged stone landscape not quite as treacherous and extreme.

After feeling safe in the distance he had made, Jaesyk fell to the chill stone, his face against hard ground, his body left to limply succumb to the landscape, and there he questioned so many things. He became entrapped in sorrow and grew wildly within it like an invasive plant that fed on rumination. Deeper and deeper, his mind delved, becoming more and more lost to this expanse. Jaesyk ruminated on the hopelessness he felt, wishing the feeling itself would go away and leave him be or that he would simply cease to exist so he no longer felt or thought anything at all. For the second time, he found himself envious of Cerutam, whose afterlife had been fully ended and whose corpse was now a part of the very structure that was the outer main wall surrounding Tartarus. A lucky outcome, deemed Jaesyk, who wished nothing more than to truly die. To no longer feel the sorrow that was drowning him.

He ruminated on how much time and energy he had wasted in this narrow-minded, hopeless, and impossible endeavor to find a way back to the living world. Realizing all the loss and pain, even the torture he had gone through thus far for this fairy-tale goal of his was nothing more than a waste—none of it worthwhile and all of it for purely nothing. His mind spiraled endlessly and oftentimes even aimlessly on all sorts of what-ifs, had-beens, and wishes for second chances to go about his time here in a different manner. A different path. Though mostly, his mind was consumed with rumination regarding one more specific thing: the End Realm itself, Hades, and why it was the way it was.

Jaesyk had lost track of time. He was growing so entrenched in depression that he no longer knew how long he had been lying there on the stone. Lost track of how long it had been since he last stood up on his own two feet even. Every so often, he would ponder how long it had been. Had he been lying in this one spot of this wasteland for days? *No*, he thought, *it's had to be weeks by now*. Or had it possibly been months? He admitted to himself that he'd lost complete bearing on time. In actuality, Jaesyk had remained fairly motionless on this small section of mostly flat obsidian for seventy-three days. And he would continue to lie there, unwilling and unable, for another three.

The vastness of the expanse he had fallen and grown into was indescribable. Only souls who've known and lived through the deepest possible depression truly know how severe the pain of such empty void and hollowness is and can know what the soulless known as Jaesyk was then going through and feeling.

The rumination he spent so much time in—why the afterlife was the way it was—became all-encompassing, and that he currently had no true way of getting the questions he posed and ruminated on answered only intensified his spiral. He continually asked himself how and why the afterlife was filled with so much vileness and evils. He could not fathom why such a cruel and unnecessary entity such as Hihliah the Devourer was allowed to walk the End Realm. A being who was torturing innocent souls, torturing them to prod and coax wishes out of them. Wishes for the pain to stop. Wishes for their afterlife to end. Wishes for someone to save them. All done so she could then feast on the wish—eating it and then regurgitating an ill omen, as if the tortured soul didn't already have enough ill fate by being the fairy demon's prisoner.

Jaesyk spent months thinking on such things, and it only made him grow angrier and sadder. Angry at Hades, the supposed leader and most powerful of the realm, the one that even the Originals called their god. If this Devil-God was so powerful and such a grand leader of the afterlife, then why had he turned a blind eye to such immense cruelty in his realm? Or is it that he wasn't turning a blind eye, but encouraged such horrific doings?

Jaesyk knew he did not have the answers he so desperately wanted. And he knew he would likely never know. In this abyssal depression, this pit of sorrow he had fallen into, knowing he would likely never know did not stop him from obsessing over such questions. In fact, knowing he may never know acted as a fuel to obsess over it even further.

Further.

And further.

Until his seventy-sixth day spent on that chilled stone ground, when his rumination was interrupted by a visitor.

A shadowy raven made an agile landing on the cold stone a few feet from the walker's head.

It cawed as it set foot, offering the walker a slight head tilt before cawing again. The raven's mannerisms made Jaesyk think of Karhon, which brought him a quick escape from the thought spiral he was delving into just moments before.

It cawed again. This time, as it did, the shadowy bird pecked down to grab something on the ground and with a jerk of its head tossed the object a bit closer to the walker. Jaesyk, still lying on the black stone, half his face pressed against it and for so long that he no longer felt the harsh chill nip at the side of his face, saw a deep bronze ring thrown from the raven's beak.

This was a familiar ring. It tinged several times across the obsidian before coming to a final low-sounding thud. The high pitch of the tings cut through the still air and the low resonance of its final rest echoed in Jaesyk's ears.

He shot up in both disbelief and confusion, wanting to give it a better look, mostly wanting to verify this was the ring he thought. It definitely was. He questioned hard in his mind, *How the fuck did this bird find this? How the fuck did it find me?*

The raven cawed again. And again. And again. Hopping a bit closer to the walker and giving purposeful stares as it did. It pecked down again and tossed the bronze jewelry closer yet, cawing aggressively this time, pointing its beak straight to the dark sky and holding its piercing song long enough that the walker winced in discomfort as the caw assailed his ears. Jaesyk took the hint and grabbed his ring from the stone as the shadowy raven bounced a couple steps backward. The two stared at each other for a moment, and the raven took a single bounce toward Jaesyk and looked up at him again. He rolled his ring around in his fingers for a moment as he inspected both it and the bird some more.

"All right." He spoke aloud for the first time in months. "Fine."

Jaesyk donned his deep bronze ring then, and something happened within. He wasn't sure if it was the raven, the ring, or maybe just his done-ness with the abyss he had been in for so long. But he knew where he was headed now, reminded of why he could not lie here and give up. The raven bounced another step closer and gave a final look to the walker and a pleasant caw before bounding off in flight.

The soulless one turned away from the bird flying off to the west and looked far north, where he could see the vast mountain in the distance. It was then that Jaesyk took his first steps in some time. To the mountain he went, the abyssal spirals left behind.

CHAPTER SEVENTEEN

Key

I 've completely lost track of time, so I am unsure how long it has taken me, but a daunting distance of obsidian and shale desert is now behind, and I think I'm now getting very close to reaching the summit of this jutting mass of stone-scape that has been my destination—Hermes Overlook.

The massive stars that were a source of daylight in the Fields of Asphodel have remained absent. The entirety of the desert— and now too this mountain—are under black skies, an endless night. I wonder if the darkness here is truly never-ending or if the day-night cycle is just so extreme that I have not been in the region long enough to witness the light of a day.

The mountain I've been ascending for what I'm guessing has to be close to two days now is exactly how Chronos described. Jagged in some areas yet smooth in others, black stone ground still lies underfoot, but the foliage on the mountain is lush and full, whereas the desert region was leafless like the area near the Deliverance Gates. Here on the mountain, every plant and tree has lush leaves or needles. Leaf colors range from dark greens to soft iridescent purples. Trees that bare needles are mostly dark, almost to the point of being black themselves; however, when inspected close enough, you can see the continuation of familiar green and purple hues, just overbearingly dark. The junipers the time warlock seemed so enamored by are unmistakable. None are very tall, but their twisted trunks and erratic branches of multiple brown tones are striking. They offer a lush low canopy that makes it feel as if I am walking through the body of some massive being—the junipers being the twisting mess of arteries and capillaries that pulse lifeblood to the entirety of the towering mountain. It's all diametric of the High Sanctum, the yin to the sanctum's yang, if you will. Though I am under endless night and surrounded by the darkest of ground and trees, there is still a great beauty and tranquility here on this mountain. And it makes me think of the beauty of Lunacrye's castle and the warmth of her air and hospitality.

Just when I think the ascent is without end, a final switchback leads me up and over the immense mileage I have managed to surmount. The view is . . . breathtaking. I had no idea the mountain was this high.

Is there trickery to this ledge?

Stepping farther onto the massive shale shelf of the overlook, I feel I can see farther than conceivably possible. Looking out to the south—back in the direction I came all this distance—I can see the Tarr Mire bordering the desert. After focusing on that border, I get the sensation that I can scan even farther. "There!" I say aloud, even pointing in the far skies. "That's—holy fuck. That's the fields . . . and the High Sanctum."

How the hell can I see all of this? There's no way . . .

I take a step back, give a hard blink, shaking my head as I hold my eyes closed. Then I look back up to the horizon to see if my eyes were playing games with me. Sure enough, off on the far horizon to the southeast, I can again make out the sanctum jutting up to the sky. A sunlit sky. "What in the hell is this? How can I see so much?"

"Um, hey, um . . . Excuuuuse me," says a bouncy shrill voice.

My heart leaps, shoulders clench, my heels leave the shale— or maybe they sink *into* the shale. I catch myself quickly, then dart my eyes over to what I can only describe as a gnome? The gnomish figure is small, standing *maybe* up to my knee height. He has short spiked hair and wears only a pair of shorts made of what looks like some sort of finely crafted linen, possibly silk. His physique is thin yet toned—muscular. And his bare feet shine a glowing white, as if they are covered in a thousand brilliant diamonds.

"Fuck!" A hand rises to my chest. "You startled the hell outta me, damn it."

"Mmm." The small man purses his lips and raises his eyebrows as his hands hold his hips, elbows out, and he begins tapping one of his bright dazzling feet on the ground as if not entertained by my jest nor satisfied with my lack of answer. My lack of answer to a question that was not necessarily asked but that he clearly felt implied. He stands there waiting.

I take an audible breath. "So, uh—" I abruptly stop. My brow furrows, and a realization hits me. "Wait. You're Hermes?" I question and point.

The tapping foot comes to a sudden halt, and his eyebrows dive from their raised post.

"Oh, no, no, NO!" he shoots, shaking a finger my way. "Don't call me that." His voice continues in the bouncy shrillness I first heard, but there's also a cheerful playfulness about him. "Call me Messenger."

"Messenger?"

"Yes, yes, yes. That's what you'll call me," he speaks fast yet clear. "That's what everyone calls me!"

"Oh. Okay, then." I toss my hands out to the side in pleasant surrender. "But you *are* Herm—" I catch myself. "Like, you're the one who talks to Hades often and can travel at great speeds?"

"Pffft." He scoffs. "What in the hell ya think I do with these bad boys?" He lifts a glowing white foot and wags it at me, giving a gnomish giggle.

"Well, yeah. I mean, if I'm telling the truth, the feet are definitely what made me realize it might be you. I actually traveled all this way to find you."

Hermes sneakily glides a bit closer, almost in a crouch, and shoots curious eyes up at me. "What do you mean, 'all this way'?" he asks, raising a single eyebrow this time. "And you say to find *me*?"

For the next hour, Hermes and I speak about much. He's very intrigued by my visit and has great curiosity about where I have come from and the "adventurous tale," as he puts it, that I have accumulated along the way to his overlook. I feel comfortable with this tiny gnomish man and basically divulge everything to him. Well, everything except how I ended Tritang while in the Lowest, as I feel that may dissuade the messenger from possibly helping me. I tell him of my time with Lunacrye and how we used one of my truth coins in the ritual. How I met Chronos and Michael, which was how I had learned of his location and his interactions with the Devil-God. And how my other truth coin was stolen from me while making my way through the Tarr Mire.

I can both see and feel Hermes's empathy, especially about the loss of the coin. He tells me how the Tarr Mire is one of the few regions of the realm where such harsh evils reside and how he long ago figured Hihliah was either an entity the Devil-God was unable to destroy for some reason or possibly unwilling. He's not certain of the details. However, he says that many of the inhabitants of the mire are physically unable to leave, bound and entrapped there by some unknown force. And most everyone else knows to stay out.

The messenger sits upright and is caught in everything I have to say. It seems every small story I tell of my journey here has

182

him on the edge of his seat. He soon asks what I feel he could do to help. I feel awkward asking and stumble on the words but manage well enough: I ask about a possible audience with Hades and if he could orchestrate that, if he knows of any other way for me to get back to my living world, and if he has any idea if there's something else Hades may take in payment for help or answers now that I'm without a truth coin.

A short silence fills the air as he sinks back a bit.

Hermes never loses his playful attitude or his fast and bouncy voice, though I can see the bounding excitement and intrigue he previously had fall some after I pose my hope for help. A slight dolefulness shows through, and his glittering diamond-covered feet seem to dim a touch. He explains that he cannot help with any issues I have brought forth. The reasoning varies. One he simply is unable to do, as other forces or rules are in control. One he states is impossible, and another, he says he simply does not know. He finishes after his explanations by saying he feels bad and wishes he could help and that from everything he's heard of my story, he does feel there is something special and abnormal about my situation here in the End Realm.

"I think the boatman was right, Jaesyk." Hermes lofts his voice as he stands, brushing off the back of his shorts. "I don't think you're supposed to be here either. So odd. Yes, odd. So very odd for someone to have lost memories. Even soulless ones enter the realm with their pasts, ya know?"

I hear him, though find myself distracted by the view—the magical arcane view Hermes's little spot on this mountain offers, where vision is boundless. *Where the fuck am I going to go now? What the hell am I going to do? I have no further leads on ways to exit this damned place.*

I let the focus of my eyes be taken by the magic of the overlook. I push my vision west through the obsidian desert. Through the vast black stone, I scan. Farther and farther west, I push into the unknown. My eyes are suddenly engulfed by greens. My eyes enter something other than the desert, but my vision is scanning so fast that the greens are all blurred—out of focus. I stop the push west and back up, adjusting my telescoping view far enough back to see the desert again, hoping to see more clearly what lies beyond the western border of the black stone.

"Ah, there it is."

"Wait, huh? Huh?" Hermes speeds through his words. "Whatcha see? Whatcha lookin' at?"

"Would you fuckin' chill, man?" I chortle. "What's this massive forest that rides the west border of the desert? It looks fricken huge!"

"Pffft." Hermes scoffs in his familiar playful tone. "Oh, you don't want to go there. There's nothing there for you."

"Pffft yourself, ya little shit," I shoot back with a laugh. "What the fuck is in there?"

Hermes goes silent and starts tugging on me to get me to come out of the magical vision. I let myself pull back from the view of the immense forest and look down to the gnome. He's looking up at me, shaking his head.

"No, Jaesyk. No one goes in there."

The messenger walks back to where we were sitting before and plops himself down again, cross-legged. I sit next to him, feeling he may decide to divulge more.

"That is the Conifer Expanse. It is a massive area of mossy forest. You see, it was once filled with souls. Birds and deer, frogs and snakes, even orcs and other humanoids called it home."

Hermes's demeanor changes entirely, as if he is not inviting conversation, but rather telling a profound and dramatic story. This time, he has caught me. I sit in silence, and intrigue washes over.

"The story is vast. Oh yes. Vast, vast indeed. But I will tell it with as much precision as I can."

His voice, for the first time, falls slow. Less bouncy. And even soft.

"See, there is an Original. Her name is Athena—one of Hades's greatest of warriors. She was wedlocked with another woman named Medusa. Though Medusa was no warrior like her wife, she had other grand strengths and powers. And she was said to have the most beautiful face in the entire universe. I know . . . Crazy to think it, yes? But it is true. It really, really is, I tell you. I saw Medusa many times. And she truly was the most gorgeous face I—or anyone else—had ever seen! Well . . ."

Hermes swallows hard and clears his throat with a gentle cough.

"Many centuries—or gosh, I bet it's been thousands of centuries by now. Anyway, a very long time ago, Athena was called to take her armies to the Old Forest—also known as the Conifer Expanse. There had been accounts of certain evils invading the forest. Evils that did not have permission from the Devil-God to enter that area of the realm, so he sent his greatest warrior and her armies to send the evils back whence they came and bring a final end to any evils that did not abide. Athena was gone from her home in the upper plains for far longer than she thought she would be, and Medusa grew fearful, sad, and lonely. Some terrible—and I mean terrible, terrible—soul started a rumor that eventually reached Medusa's ears that Athena had committed adultery while at war with the evils. It wasn't true, of course! It wasn't!"

He raises his voice slightly at this and, for the first time while sharing the tale, makes eye contact with me. "Athena was one of pure heart. Yes, yes, she had a brutal and fierce heart; she was a warrior after all. But pure and loyal. This is true!"

His speech slows again as he looks back to the ground.

"Medusa heard of this and was beyond broken. Her heart tore. She fell into a deep sadness and then quickly grew *angry*. She lashed out—retaliated—by committing adultery herself while Athena was still away."

I let out a long sigh. "Fuck . . . Hermes, that is terrib—"

185

"Don't-call-me-that!" His fast speech returns in an instant and so does that pointed finger of his. "And-don't-interrupt-me! Can't ya see I'm telling a story here?"

After it's evident that I have shut my damned mouth, he settles, shifting his bottom back and forth a bit on the shale, getting back into his previous comfort.

"Jeesh . . . Anyway, Athena returned mere weeks later. She became completely enraged at Medusa and berated her about how childish she'd been and how infuriated she was that she had not only believed her to be disloyal, but did not wait for her return to confront her about it. Instead, she'd scorned Athena and made her hurt. All on rumors alone.

"Athena truly was enraged, so enraged that she wasted no time in making the very rash decision to curse her wife. Using her demigod powers, she cast a curse on Medusa, a curse that made anyone who ever looked at her beautiful face turn to stone, their soul ending within seconds." Hermes raises a hand and snaps his fingers. "The curse took hold on Medusa immediately, and hundreds of souls that were in the audience during the dispute turned to ashen stone, their afterlives irreversibly ending.

"You see, Medusa—at her heart—was a good woman, a good soul. She couldn't bear the thought of ending anyone else, so she ran as fast she could thousands of miles, straight to the Old Forest, where she drove every other soul out and exiled herself there. For eternity."

I watch Hermes as he tells the story. I can see even now, after so many years have passed, the sadness of the tale still stings him deeply. I choose not to say anything, as I don't want to further interrupt, and I, too, find myself feeling a deep sadness. For Athena's hurt and loss. For Medusa's self-hatred and regret. For the many souls that unknowingly doomed themselves with just a single innocent look at the most fair and beautiful face in all the universe. It's so tragic. I can't imagine how lonely Medusa feels right now—having not spoken to or seen anyone in ages. To be in self-exile for so long. I pity her.

"So, yes, Jaesyk, no one—*no one*—goes in there. I do not believe a single soul has set foot in that forest since she made it her own. It is certain suicide."

Again, I find myself hearing the messenger, but my mind is elsewhere. Something has come to me—a thought, a possible key.

"Hey, Messenger."

"Yeee-ah? What is it?" he slowly replies, still rooted in the sadness of the tale.

"Is Medusa an Original too?"

"Oh yes. Yes." His speech bounces again with a bit of enthusiasm. "Yup. The two, Athena and Medusa. Yup, yup, both Originals."

A smirk comes across my face, and a breathed laugh exits my nostrils. Hermes tilts his head, scrunching his eyebrows in confused wonder at my smile and sudden changed attitude.

"What are you on about now?" he questions.

"Oh, I know how I'm going to get Hades's attention." I stand, still adorned with my pursed-lip smile, and wink down at the small gnome, who is casting a bewildered look at me while shaking his head in confusion. "I'm going to end that fucking curse."

"Oh?" the messenger asks in snide unbelievability, hands back on his hips, elbows out. "And just how? Just how, Jaesyk?"

"I'm going to kill her."

CHAPTER EIGHTEEN

Noose

A s I get within a few steps of the harsh lined border between the desert and the dense forest of rising conifers, I hear a familiar and now aggressive caw. The raven has been following me high in the sky for miles but kept its distance until now. It only makes sense that this is the same corvid that somehow retrieved my ring and returned it home, and the aggressive caws cast at me as the bird comes to a heavily guarded stance at the edge of the forest are all too familiar and confirm it.

I stop, sigh, and throw my hands out to my sides as the raven tracks back and forth on the black stone ground, feathers puffed and wings shouldered out.

"What is it now?" I shout in annoyance.

The raven's caw halts, but it keeps pacing back and forth in front of me, stopping every so often to dash me a sharp glance and head tilt. Even though the skies are a dark hollowness here, the raven's eyes still somehow catch and refract a glimmer, as if a long distant light is still reaching them, glancing off the orbs in a spectacular way.

I don't have time for this—or any other distractions, for that matter. I start a forceful march to enter the towering trees

189

and green underbrush. The raven starts its raucous screaming instantly and manages to make itself look even a little bigger by widening its wings—but still in a shouldered manner. Its pace is no longer walked, but hopped, showcasing further urgency.

Goddammit.

"What?!" I shout, bending down over the annoying bird in intimidation and an attempt to convey my hurried nature. "Who are you and what the hell do you want?"

A series of caws rings out as the corvid eyes me at changing angles, though the caws feel distant this time and quickly become overlapped by a shriek-like bird voice playing inside my head.

"Caw." *I'm Ohgmay, the eyes, ears, and voice of this land . . .* the raven says. *Nothing enters here any longer. The conifers harbor someone unsafe.* "Caw."

My towering posture over the bird cripples, and I step back. "Whoa, you can fucking talk?"

No response.

"I know of the dangers. I know Medusa is the only one in the forest, and that's actually why I'm here. I need to find her. Maybe you can help?" After I pose my question, the raven, Ohgmay, rests their feathers and stands tall to look up at me. I sense a hint of confusion from the bird.

"Caw." *Nothing enters any longer. You shouldn't go.* "Caw."

The raven swings their entire head from side to side, pointing their beak as they stretch their neck each time to shake their head in an overly exaggerated no.

"Yeah, see," I explain, "I *am* entering the forest, and I will seek out Medusa until I find her. I hear your warning, but it will not stop me. She is someone I must find, and I suspect with such keen eyes and ears, you could guide me in the right direction."

Ohgmay shakes their head again, gesturing a repeated no.

"Caw." *You shouldn't go.* "Caw."

I lower myself down, bringing myself into a kneeling position on the stone, wanting to be on the same level as the shadowy raven. "Ohgmay, I need your eyes, ears, and your voice to guide me to my destination. I can tell you know where she is. Maybe we can offer each other a trade. What would you need from me to lead me to the cursed one?"

The raven steps closer, eying me curiously from as many angles they can. After their curious investigation of many odd glances and agile head tilts, Ohgmay comes up and pecks at my deep bronze ring.

"Caw." *Trade for the gold piece, the ring.* "Caw."

I stare down at my hand and the ring that Ohgmay pecks gently and tastes a few more times. Thoughts and emotions come, but it feels right. It feels okay.

"Caw." *Before, it was not mine to take.* "Caw."

"Where I am going, feathered one, I do not think I will be needing this." I thoughtfully remove the ring, spin it between my fingers a moment, and hold it out for the telepathic raven. They caw gently and low, almost in a purr, and slowly pluck it from my palm.

The raven bounces and hops, seeming to have caught a touch of excitement.

"Caw." *She is deep in the conifers, a cave!* "Caw."

I stand. "Okay." I brush off my hands. "Let's go."

Ohgmay caws several times, the echoes of their brash chorus seem to sing from the very stone beneath and too from the mile-high trees ahead.

"Caw." *Follow.* "Caw."

The shadow leaves the cold black stone and flies to the harsh line of forest that abruptly ends the desert.

"Caw." *Keep up!* "Caw."

✪ ✪

"Hey!" I call out between heavy breaths. "Hey! Would you stop for just one damned second?"

I want to stop so damn bad. Hours and hours of constant running, darting between the fairly evenly spaced mile-tall trees, jumping over occasional forest debris, pushing through patches of large dense ferns—it has all taken a toll on me, and a short rest is all I can think of. Unfortunately, the raven has been unrelenting in their forward ambition.

I stop running and hunch over with deep breaths, hands on my knees in protest. "This damned bird . . ." I whisper.

Ohgmay caws as they end flight and perch on a high branch in the distance, just barely visible, nearly out of range. I stand and start walking, making my break quick as I'm sure they are moments from bounding off and onward again. Though as my advance continues, Ohgmay remains silent, waiting. A golden light begins to rise on the horizon. It casts itself through the trees and glistens off low-growing ferns covered in slick dew. These golden rays bring me a renewed breath of life. A morning! The beginning of a day's light! The shadowy raven is a ways ahead yet and still perched on one of the only horizontal tree limbs in view. Most of the Conifer Expanse thus far has been nothing but vast tree trunks that soar high into the darkness above, not many having outward branching limbs this low near the forest floor. The bird's black silhouette against the rising golden rays makes for a poetic and beautiful scene. My pace becomes a run, and the breathless tiredness fades as a smile sneaks across my face. I bound forward.

"Ohgmay! It's a morning! A day has begun, and there is light, look!"

It seems like an entire era has passed since I last saw the light of a nearby star in the skies. Immense miles and time has passed since the brightly lit days in the Fields of Asphodel. In this moment, all is forgotten. As I rush to Ohgmay, my mind is cleared. It is not on returning to Nahla or ending Medusa or anything else. I am simply *being* in the morning light. And feeling possibly . . . yes, possibly *happiness*.

I get under the tree where Ohgmay is perched, the golden light of the coming day so bright that my eyes can now only see the raven as a pure black silhouette. The ring that was once mine dazzles brightly in their beak as they caw. I laugh aloud and spin in a circle with my arms spread as wide as they'll go. "Are you seeing this, Ohgmay?" I let out a lofty breath, chuckling some more, relishing in the golden morning rays.

The silhouette caws again as Ohgmay bounds from their high perch and crosses the morning air right over my head. Ohgmay gets so close in their swoop over me I swear I feel the gentle graze of a wing or bony foot breeze through my hair. They land across the way atop a small rock outcropping. Caws again.

And again.

The smile that came when my breathlessness faded now fades too. The short-lived forgetfulness of where I am and why I'm here crashes and shatters on the rocks upon which Ohgmay stands, for a darkened black hole at the center of the outcropping of rocks swallows any light that dares to try to reach it. I wish in this moment that I could stay in the morning light. *Damn how I want to stay.* I know I can't though. This is what I have come for. I let that wish pass.

The cave seems to swallow the ambient sounds of the old forest as everything falls to near silence. Ohgmay caws, which I can hear as it pierces through the tightly thin air, though any echo of the raven's call that would have been is consumed by the dark depths. They fly a short distance to another rock among the many that encircle the black hole that is the cave entrance, giving me curious looks and tilts of their tactile neck.

My mood shifts not to sad or frightened, but to committed. I set forth into the cavern with my eyes pinned on the ground so as not to be turned to stone. As I cross into the black hole, letting the golden light behind me suffocate, I hear Ohgmay's gentle feet click lightly against the stone above and then the flutter of their shadowy wings as they bound away.

The cavern floor is damp. I can hear water dripping off stalactites and finding rest on the stone floor. The air so silent in this space. I hear my breathing as it echoes across the moist underground walls. I know not how deep the cave goes, nor the proximity of any terrain features, and I fight the urge to bring my eyes off the ground to gain my bearings. I slowly step farther into the dark gray lightness of the cave; my eyes must have adjusted somehow. It's not nearly as black and consuming as it appeared from outside. I stop, close my eyes. *You've got this.* I take a slow deep breath, exhaling even slower, and grab Karhon's onyx dagger from its sheath at my side, and in the silence of the cavern, I scream as loud as my voice allows.

"MEDUSAAA!" I hold the scream out as long I can, giving pause after. The cavern sounds immense. The shallow echoes are heard drifting and bouncing off walls and tunnels far, far from where I stand.

"Cursed one!" I exclaim. "Show yourself!"

After each echo settles, only silence seems to remain. I carefully step farther into the cavern. I hear something shift ahead to my left. I freeze. I grip my left hand into a fist a few times, making sure I'm frozen by choice and not turning to stone. It's footsteps. They start off soft and slow but turn to a heavy fallen run. Instinctually, my eyes dart up! My right hand grips the metal hilt of Karhon's dagger even tighter. Long red hair sways in the air of the cavern as petite bare feet slap the wet surface of the cave's floor.

"Stop!" I yell.

The figure ahead halts. Then a hiss startles me in my ear. I jump and look beside me into the darkness. Something slides across the floor away from me. I barely make out the tail of a snake as it finishes slithering behind a wide stalagmite to my right. Afraid to lose track of the red-haired woman, I quickly peel back in that direction to find her turned and looking straight at me. My eyes go wide, and I become dazed in both disbelief and awe. The fiery-haired woman has flowing locks that careen down to her hips. Her high cheekbones, artful jaw, citrine eyes, and olive skin make for the fairest face I have ever seen. She is even more beautiful than Arch-Sorceress Lunacrye.

A sudden shock comes over the woman as she startles and rushes both hands up, covering her heavy gasp.

"Who—" She stops herself mid-speech by covering her lips. "Who?" she begins again, covering her mouth in shock. "Who are you?"

I take a moment to look around me and back at the stalagmite where the snake escaped to. The cavern is low-ceilinged but wide and looks to flow deeper in the direction the woman is. A bewildered feeling rushes me. I find myself taken aback and confused as to why I haven't been turned to stone in my mistake and ill willpower in keeping my eyes snared to the ground. So clearly, this woman is not the cursed one. But then why would she be here in the Old Forest and this cave? I look back to the woman, who still has her hands clasped to her mouth.

"Uh, I am here to . . ." I pause and trail off a bit, cautiously choosing what to and how much to divulge. "Find someone."

She remains still in her place but brings her hands down slightly to her shallow dainty chin. "It is just me," the woman says. "I . . . I am the only one to find here."

Again, I'm checking my surroundings, looking around, feeling confused, not sure what to think. Also feeling a breadth of displacement and fear of the darkness around me. I double-check the stalagmite again.

"I am here to find a cursed woman. Medusa. I was led here by—"

"That is I!" The woman takes a step toward me as she gasps again, clutching her mouth, wide-eyed in disbelief.

"Bullshit," I state. "The cursed one turns anything to stone on sight, and . . . well, here I stand."

"No, it is the truth! I swear it. Look!"

The woman points near a wall of the cave. I squint my eyes and step a few paces closer to a rock sculpture resembling a fox or small wolf perhaps. It's riddled with small stalactites dropping from its edges, and small spots of quartz growth run across its back, marking the age of the stone formation.

"Please, come closer. I want to see that you are real," she says, her voice carrying less shock. She now sounds soft-voiced, almost with a note of pleading.

I stand strong where I am, still not fully understanding how this could be. And not wanting to fall into any sort of danger or trap. "Why is it, then, that I can look straight at you?"

The woman sighs, giving a look of sadness, but never moves her gemlike yellow eyes from mine. "My curse is absolute. This is true. The one who cursed me made sure to give it one caveat though, her way of making the curse as sick as she could, you see. She thought it would give me a glimmer of hope, in turn causing that much more pain and despair. The truth of my curse is that anything that looks me in the face turns to stone *if* I am the most beautiful face that thing has ever seen. So you see, being created with the most beautiful face in the universe is a curse in itself."

She takes another step forward and waves a pleading palm to me as she starts to cry. Gentle tears well in her citrine eyes and drift down her pretty olive skin. "Please." She sobs over her words. "Please let me touch you. Are you real?"

I grip my dagger again at my side, feeling untrusting as I remember the trickery of Hihliah in the Tarr Mire. "That still doesn't tell me why I am still standing here," I shoot with some aggression. "Able to move and speak after looking right at you and not ending up like that!" I finish, pointing to the stone canine.

"You are so rare." The woman breathes. "You are the thing the one who cursed me thought would never happen. You have, at some time, seen someone even more gorgeous than me."

"Nahla," I say. It hits me in an instant. It has to be her. It couldn't be anyone else.

"Nahla?" she questions. "Is this the name of someone you know?"

"Yes . . . She's my wife."

⊛ ⊛

Medusa and I share our stories together. She shares some loving memories she has with Athena. It's an experience hard to remain stoic through. I can see in her eyes that such memories don't just bring happiness, but also great pain and longing. Most of what she shares with me are horrific details of how she's had to watch thousands of walkers and animals—really any soul that looked at her—turn to stone and their afterlife be ripped from them without warning. It becomes clear rather quickly that Medusa's mind has succumbed to changes over the years, and it has been a *lot* of years.

I am shown what seems to be endless cavern tunnels and walls filled with numbers—the count of days. It seems the other Originals have lost track of time or lost interest in tracking time through the eons. In her self-exile though, Medusa has made it even harsher on herself by keeping track of each and every day, every year, every century. She's able to tell me she isolated herself to the Old Forest over thirteen billion years ago. The staggering number rolls off her tongue as though it is meaningless and has no weight to her. To me though, it's jaw-dropping. I cannot imagine the turmoil and despair this woman has endured. I'm stricken by it. And it feels overwhelming and exhausting to even imagine a century alone, much less hundreds of thousands of them.

I, too, share my tales, and where with Hermes I chose to skirt around some events, with Medusa, I tell all. I feel I owe her full disclosure and honesty, and I also feel I won't be judged by her—and I'm not. I feel she can understand and admire another showing their downfalls and dark times. This means she hears the truth about why I have sought her out. And what I was hoping to accomplish in doing so. Medusa nods to all of this, saying I must continue my path and that, though she does not know for certain if my actions will be significant enough to catch the attention of Hades, she feels that if they aren't, then not much else could.

She explains how she has wished for great lengths of time that her pain and loneliness would end. How she wishes the Old Forest could go back to being a place of life and beauty. How she wishes she could do something to redeem herself after the poor choices she made those eons ago when she betrayed her wife. She wishes for all these things, and while she does, I am able to see the sorrow in her eyes, but also a glimpse of freedom. And a glimpse of hopefulness for what her ending could bring.

She kisses me on the lips and brings a cold hand to the side of my face. "Thank you, Jaesyk, for sharing your tale. And for being such a greatly determined soul. The worlds and realms would be a better place with more having a heart like your own."

Tears start gleaming at the edges of her magnificent eyes. "I truly wish you the very best of luck." She strokes the back of her fingers across my cheek before lying down next to where I sit on the cavern floor. Her piles of wavy fiery red hair spread across my legs as she lays her head down in my lap. I run my hands through her hair as I pull the long strands of fire away from her fair face, taking some moments to make her hair lay nicely and wipe some of her tears away as I see them welling.

"Please," she cries in a whisper.

I can feel the years of pain seeping out of her in an aura around us as she softly weeps. The sorrow in this space and within her is immeasurable. I gently lift her head from my lap and let the side of her face down on the cold damp stone—facing away from me. I lift the onyx dagger from my side. The blood jewel set into the pommel glistens in the pale gray darkness. The liquid core of the gem weaves in somber motion, matching the cavern's tone. My other hand runs through Medusa's hair near her scalp to show her she is, for once, not alone. I breath deep. I can hear by the way she's taking breaths that she is still crying.

I know I can't do this without turning something off within me. I am too present. I care too much. The emotions knocking, pounding at my sternum—they have to be shut off if I'm to do this. I give my head a jolting shake to separate myself and bring the dagger up high. I dig my fingers down into her crimson hair, holding her beautiful skull secure against the stone. I can hear nothing now. Pure silence falls as I bring the blade down with force, cutting hard into the flesh of her neck.

Up high again I bring it, squeezing tightly her beautiful head against the stone floor and my grip on the blade.

Down!—again the blade crashes against her neck. I'm not sure if it is stone I've hit yet or more bone.

UP!—I bring the blade high again. My firm grasp against her head starts to slide from the added crimson red splashing into her hair. I let go and knot my fingers into her hair more, clenching them into a fist to get an even tighter hold against her skull.

DOWN!—again I bring the blade down into the void that was once her neck. A splash hits my face. I still hear nothing, not my breathing, not the blade against flesh, bone, or stone. My ears cease, and I let no sound in, protecting myself from what sounds may be assailing the cavern's air.

UP!—I can't stop until I know her head is free from her body. I can't stop until I know she isn't feeling anymore. I know I can't stop.

DOWN!—I bring the blade again. I keep going. I grip against her gorgeous skull tighter and tighter. I bring the blade down faster and faster each time. With each strike, more and more blood pools and spatters.

ing all around me. Deep cracks erupt, sundering the floor of the
cavern. The floor gives way and shifts. Parts of the stone floor
start completely falling away—down into some endless abyss.
I look down at the body before me. Still gripping the gnarled
and knotted crimson red mess of hair in my fist, I lift . . .

It's free.

Her head—face still looking away from me—dangles in
my grasp. The entire floor crumbles now and gives way, falling
farther and farther down into nothingness. Into black. A sudden
cinch comes abruptly around my neck—I can't breathe. I'm being
choked out by something. Something *has* me! I'm stricken with
panic as the pressure increases around my throat, trapping all the
blood pumping into my head. My face turns warm and throbs.
I lose my grip on Medusa's blood-soaked and severed head.
Along with the mass of cavern stone, it falls into the abyss below.
While I seem to stay above . . . everything seems to fall away.

The entire cavern has now fallen away from me. The grip
around my neck becomes even harsher as I'm suddenly being
pulled backward now through complete empty blackness. I
manage to stow the dagger at my side and bring up both hands,
trying to free myself from whatever has a hold on me. There is
nothing there. It feels like a noose has caught me around the
neck and is pulling me through an empty void, but I can get no
purchase on anything doing so.

A dizziness sets in—and fast.

Not able to breath and losing the strength to keep my hands
up in an attempt to free my throat, I feel myself slipping from
consciousness. The weight of my eyelids becomes like the weight
of Medusa's sorrow and pain. It overtakes . . . and I am gone.

CHAPTER NINETEEN

Throne

"Wake."

The word is faint . . . in the darkness of a dream. I try to look around, looking for something, anything tangible in the void, but nothing is here. "Wake!"

It comes denser this time as I feel my head swing abruptly to the left. Still nothing to be seen in this new direction. *Am I trapped in a dream? A nightmare? Where have I been pulled—*

"WAKE!"

The word slams against me. Pain chisels across my face. I can again feel the noose taut around my neck. My eyes flicker open briefly as if violently trying to flee from sleep. A second wave of stinging fire scorches across my face like the aftermath of being struck. I pull in as much of a gasp of air as is allowed through the tension around my neck. The struggle to breathe swirls in my stomach, arms, into my hands. I can't make it happen fast enough. *Panic.* Panic smothers and fear hits hard enough that I'm shaken awake. More by the sense of dread than even the raking of pain slashed across my face.

"You." A skeletal face before me speaks in deep searing spite. "The one who bears the disgrace of the three swords upon your hand, the mark of the Lowest." My neck is wrenched tighter as the words come. "Tell me, how does one so disgustingly unworthy get beyond Alastor's wall, remain uncaptured, and then somehow manage to slay an Original? One that's been damaged so by the Gorgon's curse. This, I ask!"

Fuck, this has to be him. The massive, overbearing in scale, darkly robed, and armored skeleton standing under me—the Devil-God, Hades, who is holding me high above, squeezing the afterlife out of me with one hand. Open palmed, his other giant hand of fleshless bone is held high, ready to rake across my face again at any moment.

I writhe in his grip, attempting to speak, to breath. The noose, which is now clearly the grasp of the Devil around my neck, causes any attempt at such to sound of meek gargling and raspy panicked gasps.

His grip becomes even tighter as his bare skull tenses, causing exposed teeth to grind hard against each other, his hollow eye sockets starting to spark with green fiendish flares of hatred and murderous disdain. I feel myself slipping again. This is it . . . The Devil-God is to end me here. The crushing of my neck sinks me further and further back into the void of unconsciousness. The weight atop my eyelids threatens to slam down into a final seal of fate.

"Darling!" an echoing feminine voice bounds from afar, shattering the tension around my neck.

The threatening weight abruptly lifts from my brow, and an instinctive lifesaving gasp rings out. Cold air wheezes through my nearly collapsed throat, shotgunning into my oxygen-deprived lungs. A heavy dizziness falls into my eyes from the rush of newfound air. Dancing sparkles of starlight rush through my vision as my body is loosed from the Devil-God's wrath.

I start falling through the air, though I never seem to reach the floor. Falling and falling, I continue, the brisk air rushing past me and through my hair. Though I felt like I was choked not ten feet from the ground, the distance I seem to fall feels overwhelming and vast. The crushing blow of dense stone finally meets my shoulder and the back of my head—ending the seeming forever free fall. The pounding footsteps from afar encroach, their vibrations reaching my bones.

"And what in the realm's name is this about, husband?"

"You need not see this, Persephone." The anger has, in an instant, left Hades's voice. And though still deeply low toned and aggressive, it becomes replaced with dire sincerity. "This soulless has defiled one of our own! Medusa has been slain, at his hands! He must answer . . . and meet demise."

Pain aches from the back of my skull and shoulder as I try to gain my bearings from my position on the floor. The dancing stars begin their departure, and my vision starts to clear fast now that my lungs are receiving what they needed most from my pleading breaths. Hades stands near, towering over me. Dark stone-armored boots and matching gauntlets adorn the Devil-God, both sharply shaped and very much like the stone and metal adornments that protected the Maw, Karhon. Long forest-green robes hang from under the god's towerlike pauldrons, reaching down to the floor before me. Loose threads, rips, and tears scatter across the ancient green material, giving the pieces of robe the look of tattered and torn drapery. Hades's skeletal head appears mostly human, though the top of his skull stands tall where weathered bone forms ridges that peak high toward the cluttered ceiling of massive candlelit chandeliers; the many bone-spiked peaks that encircle his skull resemble a treacherous crown. The bone crown of the ruler of the realm, the crown of the Devil, the crown of God, the crown of the king and ruler of the afterlife.

Persephone keeps to her approach, each footfall sending vibrations through the floor. These gods are massive, standing strikingly tall. As the woman marches farther into the room, small green plants, seedlings, and tiny flowers sprout from the stone in every space that her bare feet of rich brown skin step, as if growth and life flow from her very being. Everything in this candlelit chamber seems otherworldly—both magical and frightful to the grandest of degrees.

The walls echo again with her traveling and confident voice. "Need I still remind you after all our eons together that you need not handle certain dealings alone, husband? Now—"The trail of fertile plant life has followed her with every step and up to the quainter of two thrones set into the stonework of the floor ahead. Persephone traces her fingernails across the stonework of her throne. Lush vines crawl along the path of her nails and lance out impatiently every few inches to spread themselves with unnaturally fast growth. "Let us see to this," she finishes as she slowly sits with straight and royal posture.

Hades shoots his searing infernal gaze back at me through his hollow skull. Denser fiendish sparks erupt from where his eyes would be as he does. I can hear a low growl from within his clenched jaw as he brings one of his bone hands out toward me. I feel the noose again, though this time, it strangles my entire body as I'm forced off the floor to my feet.

"You!" he sneers. "Do not deserve the comfort of lying on this restful floor." The fiendish green within his eyes rages brighter with what feels like executioner's intent. "Stand, you pathetic waste," he finishes.

Hades walks to the two thrones standing next to each other at the back center of the room. Ghastly dark smoke billows from the seams of his vestments and black armored pauldrons, which stand tall atop his shoulders. The air and aura that exudes from the Devil-God is dominant and imposing.

He stands next to his immense sculptured throne, resting an undead skeletal hand across its back. He does not sit as his counterpart chose to, though he offers his wife a short loving bow before aiming his spiteful stare back down at me across the room. If I had a soul, I venture the very presentation and air of

Hades could cast it out of my body in fear-filled escape. There is something powerful and utterly damning in the towering gaze he sets down on me. *Into* me even.

Persephone closes her eyes and gives a short bow of her head in return to her spouse but never wavers from her courtly and proud royal posture. "Well, soulless." She speaks straight, not quite in a yell, though much louder and more direct than I expected. "Is this truth my darling husband speaks? Has our fair-faced Medusa met her end?" As she finishes, her demeanor looks to mold more and more into that of her husband's, and I now feel a near-damning gaze cast from her brow too.

The candlelight from the massive metal-casted chandeliers that pepper the variable-height ceiling flare and flicker heavily across the glossy floor—and my blood-soaked hands. Tension rips through me in waves, and hurricane-like gusts of timid insecurity hit against my ribs as I try to hold myself together the best I can. I feel as though my entirety is mere moments away from folding in on itself, though I cannot let this paralysis take hold. This is what I sought. This audience is the one I have so chased.

"It is—" I choke anxiously on the words. "It is true. Though it was of mutual desire. This I swear. She sought an end to her cursed existence, and I . . ." My eyes try best not to look too directly at the two godly beings. My head mostly points down, at their feet. "I sought an audience with the Devil-God, Hades."

"An audience with me you *have*," Hades infernally snarls. He steps forward, pointing menacingly at my waist. "That onyx blade is *not* yours to wield. How did you come by this?"

Hades marches back toward me, his sharply armored boots hitting the floor like fallen boulders with each heavy step. Panic assaults me again. I fumble for the dagger at my side, bringing it held out in surrender to the Devil bounding my way. Odd physics or magic is at play. Hades's physical size seems to change on approach. Near the thrones, he stands tall as a giant, yet as he nears, his height changes to match much closer to my own.

"Karhon of the Rivers . . ." I begin attempting to spout my tale before the Devil closes in on me. "He gifted me this before my arrival at Tartarus. He kept saying I wasn't meant to be here. See, he . . . he kept making a big deal about the two truth coins I entered with and how I didn't have memory of who I was or what my life was like before this realm. Lunacrye used one of my coins to learn of my wife, who I'm trying to get back to in the living world called Earth—"

"Enough!" Hades shouts.

He swipes the dagger from me and takes a moment to carefully look it over. A look of contemplation runs across his bone face. He turns to Persephone, who's sitting neatly, then turns back to me, his hollowed eye sockets squinting down, giving deep inspection. Hades creeps back to his immense throne that's littered with artfully set gems and stones of all sizes and hues. He holds the blade out for Persephone to see.

"Love, this is Karhon's true blade. Look." His deep devilish voice still resonates low, though when he speaks to Persephone, a soothing respect is heard within. He brings the dagger down near one of the armrests of his throne. A small empty setting is there, one shaped remarkably like the blood jewel set in the pommel of the Maw's dagger.

Persephone starts speaking to Hades but keeps her unwavering gaze on me. "Go corroborate this with your best of men, Karhon. I will watch over our guest who is not meant to be here, as he says."

"My return will be prompt," Hades says firmly as he again stands. "Find what you can. Something is amiss."

Hades holds the dagger in his skeletal hands near his sharp chin as he mutters an incantation to it. The ghastly smoke that seeps from his vestments pours out faster and encircles the

Devil-God in a swirl of black haze, which quickly fades, along with himself.

Silence quickly becomes noticeable. Persephone gleams at me, one eyebrow raised.

"So . . . a soulless with no Tartarus coin." She stands, still eying me, and slowly makes her way down the candlelit stairs of their thrones' platform. "And not one, but two coins of truth." She tosses two fingers in the air, looking at me with an almost playful and teasing eye.

"I—yes, I have tried searching for answers as to why. It doesn't seem anyone can help me understand," I stammer.

"Oh, I think it is clear. My husband is very right. Something is amiss here." She continues closer, starting to pace around me as she nears. "There is something radiating from you, soulless. Something wrong and displaced, but also something . . . potent, powerful, and familiar-r." She trails off in playful curiosity.

The valiant woman has a presence of caregiving and an air of soothing that weaves from her space. She does not strike fear in me, though she does not bring with her the gentle air of safety that emanated from Lunacrye. The trail of seedlings and tiny flowers that find root in her every step now circles me, and she finishes her walk of inspection, standing almost too close, my comfort waning a touch. Her soft brown near-black skin glows almost bronze in the flickering chandelier light. Her hazel eyes flecked with small shards of emerald green help me find that touch of lost comfort.

"Your name?" Persephone beckons.

"Jaesyk. Or soulless, miss. Whichever you prefer."

The raw power within the chamber ceases any confidence or strength I had before. Here, I am nothing more than an insect. A mere dot. A grain of sand amongst titans.

Persephone places her finger to my chest. "Oh, Jaesyk." She smiles. "I think I've found that potent familiarity."

Her finger presses harder against my chest. Then even harder as I feel her fingernail just start to give the sensation of piercing against my skin. I look up at her, brow furrowed in a look of question. Her warm gentle smile has faded into a look of gravity. A sudden jolt hits me as she thrusts her fingers—like knives—into my chest. I look down, perplexed and in shock. Her hand is pierced through me, wrist deep, and my warm blood pools out around her petite soft bronze wrist, making a crimson bracelet. I feel her straight fingers clench hard in a fist as she grabs firmly within. Then she tears her grip from my opened chest. A mist of red fog follows her hand's retreat. The light spray of blood feels like a soft breeze across my bare neck. I reach up, fearfully grabbing at the massive open wound to close it off and prevent myself from losing more blood. As I haphazardly and anxiously try to close the gaping wound, I realize there is no pain, no tempting loss of consciousness, or even the feeling of death. I look back up to her in awful perplexed surprise. My beat-less and bloody heart is held in her grasp.

"Shhh," she hushes to me with a finger against her lips. "I have done no real harm, I promise, but look, soulless . . . See? You have the heart of a champion, a knight, a scorpion even. A heart like this is a blessing and a curse—my favorite kind of heart." Persephone tosses a sly wink at me, blood still dripping from the lifeless heart she holds. "Not unlike the Devil-God's own heart, you see."

"How . . . how is this painless?" I ask, looking down at my blood-soaked palms and the cavity in my chest.

Persephone's smile returns, and then a loud almost maniacal hearty chuckle ensues, hauntingly ricocheting across the chamber walls. "Oh, I have my ways."

My knees are locked in place, my mind in shock, with no real clue as to how to proceed in this chaotic and surreal experience I find myself in.

"You will be fine, Jaesyk. I have had a very long time to master my intuition and am grateful to have succeeded in doing just that. I know an incredible heart when I see one. My husband is a lot of things to the extreme, untrusting being one of them. You'll see, dear. Once he knows the unknown, his attention on you will flip like night and da—"

She cuts herself short, looking back near the thrones as a rushing cloud of wraithlike umbra swirls, revealing Hades returned to the chamber.

"Ah, darling!" she says cordially.

My red hands have thickened and begun to crack, leaving tiny flesh-colored trails through the drying blood, resembling a scorched desert. I find myself perplexed by Persephone's excitement at her husband's return. She's speaking as if there is something new and amazing to share. *As if there is nothing abnormal or troublesome about a vital organ being ripped from my chest. What the fuck.*

"Look at this," she says, making her walk to the Devil-God.

She meets her husband where he's emerged from his devilish teleportation spell. He notes the carried heart as she gets in close to him and begins speaking softly so only they can hear. Hades looks down at my now displaced heart as she speaks, then slowly up to me.

"Sit, dear." He beckons her, raising a hand gesturing to her throne.

The wife of Hades returns to her posture of royalty, my heart resting in her palms upon her lap, paying no mind to the crimson hue now staining her gown.

"Karhon's dagger, which was a gift from me, has been returned," the Devil-God says while bringing his hands to a restful state behind his lower back.

He starts to advance my way, though he now levitates slightly off the floor rather than walking like a mere mortal, his sharp bone chin now in a higher prouder presentation, his plated chest armor and towering pauldrons seeming more rigidly worn, matching his Godlike posture. Hades drifts until he's right before me, floating inches off the chamber floor. My breath is stolen, his proximity pushing a frigid air straight through my bones. I want to speak, to plead my case and ask what I came here to ask. His presence though, it *crushes* down on me, making even words difficult to craft.

I look up, meeting the blink-less stare of his hollow eyes a good two feet above my own, the frigid radiation shedding from where he stands still reaching my bones and effortlessly passing through the carved hole in my chest, bringing me to a noticeable shiver.

"Karhon," Hades says with power, "has been a loyal confidant and the grandest of friends since the very beginning of my time. I trust in him as deeply as I trust in my Persephone."

Through his words, Hades stands still, holding his proud posture. The scorn toward me has now noticeably left his booming icy voice.

"He has validated certain accounts of your tale," he says as his back turns, making his way once more toward his throne. "And my most powerful of time warlocks has done the same with some missing pieces I wished to see."

The Devil-God takes his place upon the vast jewel-set throne. Skeletal hands gripping the ends of the marble-orbed armrests, he pushes himself forward to be at the very edge of his stone seat and directs an over-the-brow glare into me.

"So, soulless, what is it you want?"

Just as warmth started to enter my spine, since the frigid aura followed Hades back to his throne, cold sets in harsh again as my stomach drops. Hades glares, awaiting my response. Awaiting a response that feels impossible to give in this crushing environment.

I clear my throat, but the hard swallow does little. I stammer. "I seek—erm—I seek to be—to be back with my wife in the living world I was born into. I made promises to her. I feel I have broken a promise by leaving her side, even if it was by death and not my own doing."

"And, soulless, who says you've died?" Hades impugns curiously.

"I . . . I don't know what you mea—"

"It matters not either way, however!" Hades interrupts and sits back, slouching into his throne. "Deliverance into this realm is finality. Exit is near impossible. And"—Hades raises and tosses a hand, as if resigning the notion of something—"what payment you did possess has been taken, has it not? And even more payment would be needed after beheading the cursed one, even if a true end *was* what she wished from you."

Hades pauses, long. The sound of bone knocking against stone echoes in the silence as the Devil-God thrums his fingers in waves against the marble orb at the end of an armrest. The two immortal partners turn heads to look at each other. The thrumming of bone fingers comes to a smooth stop as the two gods look into each other's eyes for what seems an awkward length of time before Hades's stare leaves Persephone's and drifts down to the coagulated heart resting in her lap. The two look directly at me together.

"There is a way, soulless." Hades's deep voice goes shallow, almost to an airy ghostly whisper. "Though even I have limitations. Such a breaking of the universe's rules would require a grand price. The universe will not allow me to make a mockery of its planar physics without *an exchange*."

"I will hear it! What can I pay?" I say loud and pleadingly as I kneel to the ground in surrender.

"STAND!" Hades booms so loud the very foundation of the chamber shakes.

My second knee hasn't yet hit the floor before I am startled straight to my feet, eyes wide and stunned at Hades's display of discontent. He's now standing and enormously postured.

He breathes heavily through his skeletal neck as he looks to try to settle his displeasure. "Your end crime against Medusa has not been forgotten. You are not to sit, lie, or kneel upon this stone."

"Understood." I bow my head in as much of an apology as I can gather myself to do, keeping eyes to the floor.

"I will send you back through the veil, though a favor is owed, soulless." The Devil-God takes a grand breath, exhaling steady and slow—the sound of a winter wind through a cage of bones. "Upon your return to this realm, you will seek an audience with me once again, and I will ask this favor of you at that time."

Hades waits.

I look around while thoughts dash through my mind. Persephone still sits straight and proud in her throne, her eyes on me. Hades stands tall, hands resting in front of him with fingertips meeting. The many chandeliers above cast a thousand flickers of candlelight down on them like rain—the rain of heaven and hell. Insects of fear make their return, along with uncertainty. But I also feel passion and an anxious thrill! *Did I hear him right? He said he could get me back, but is this a trick? Ah, fuck. Even if it is, this is the end of the road. There's no other end goal. This was fucking it. An audience with Hades was it, and here I am.*

"How will I get an audience with you after my return here?" I cautiously ask.

The fiendish spark and fire flares slightly in the Devil-God's eyes. "Evidence demonstrates your resourcefulness, soulless. I believe you will find a way." He towers his aggressive sneering gaze down on me. "Trust in me. It is better you come my way than I yours . . ."

I nod. "Okay. An unsaid favor is the favor I'll owe you on my return. I swear it." I say, sealing the deal with the Devil.

Hades brings out a pentacle talisman from around his neck, which has been hidden under his chest plate. With a flick and a ting, the metal talisman is sent spinning as he holds it up by the attached silver chain necklace.

"Azrael, come to me," Hades mutters at the talisman.

Across the chamber, an oozing black oil starts bubbling and roiling from the floor. As it froths and bubbles over on itself, more and more, the thick tar-like oil grows and bulges into a heaping slick mass. The mass flows and wraps around on itself and starts contorting, as if trying to force and mold itself into something other than its current state. The tar eventually forms itself into a jet-black Friesian stallion. The Friesian drips glossy oil from its mane that sizzles and steams into nothingness as it hits the throne room's floor. The stallion nods and throws its head in greeting as it neighs and hoofs the smooth stone.

"Azrael," the Devil-God addresses the horse. "Guide this one back through the veil. Their mortal shell has yet to take its last breath."

Azrael stretches his front hooves out, bowing low.

"You will be needing this." Hades brings to me the heart that was once within my chest. "And this, soulless." He holds out his palm, where a gold forged key materializes.

I look to Hades, not knowing what to say. Or if anything should be said at all.

Azrael's hooves clop against the stone on his way to me. I run an open palm under his eye and across his large cheek and jaw.

He is eager and waits for nothing. He bounds away through the chamber, through the walls, through anything in our way with me on his back. I cradle my heart in one arm while the other holds tight against Azrael, keeping my balance the best I can as we make haste. Everything around us becomes a blur. Azrael speeds through terrain as if the entire realm bends to his will. A journey that would have taken me endless days of travel and many unfortunate trials and tribulations takes us mere hours.

Up I look and side to side. The familiar wall before us is endless in every direction, with no escape. I look straight ahead at the damning Gothic carved black metal doors that stand stories tall. Azrael's hooves clop on our slow and closer approach to the gates. The steed stops and tosses his head some, gesturing to the Deliverance Gates. As I bring the golden key out, it glimmers in the darkness before dissolving into a million tiny dust particles that careen and swirl in a small golden cloud above my hand. The cloud shoots itself through the air, diving into the golden keylock affixed to the massive black doors.

The doors disappear in a single blink. What shows through is a dense starlit view of endless galaxies and nebulae. Azrael rears up, high, letting out an excitable neigh. *This is it* . . . I grit my teeth and hold on with all my strength—gripping both my heart and the stallion. The Friesian sets down and bolts forward harder than any time before. He charges us onward through the veil.

⊕ ⊕

Persephone looks to her beloved. "So you feel the same? You believe this one's heart is worthy enough, both as ruthless and merciful as one's needs to be to sit on the throne?"

"I do not hold any faith in belief, darling. You know this."

Persephone gives a snide eye roll, but it's loving and playful enough.

"But I hope it is. You know how tired my heart has become over the eons. Time will tell if he is worthy enough, and we can only hope this Nahla of his is worthy of your place as well. I will not let go unless we can go together."

CHAPTER TWENTY

End

eet, deet . . . Deet, deet . . . Deet, deet . . .
I hear a clear continuous cadence sounding like medical monitors of some sort, but everything is pitch-black, much like the pierce chamber. I feel no physical sensation of any kind. It's concerning. Did I make it? Or did something go wrong? Do I even reside in a physical body? Are my eyes open? Closed?

Deet, deet . . . Deet, deet . . .

I hear a muffled voice, and at the same time, I gain some mobility and the sense of touch in what feels like a hand . . . in what feels like my own hand.

A blurry white circle starts to expand exponentially in the center of my black vision, eventually clearing the pitch-black void. I can see. *I think.*

Looking down, I indeed see. And I can now move the hand that I was gaining feeling back into. And as soon as my mind concludes that, that's when I see her getting up from a chair in which she had been sitting. She stares at me and looks fallen, almost like she's staring straight through my eyes into the mad wonder of disbelief.

"Jaesyk . . ." she says almost under her breath as she turns and heads to a glass door directly behind and to her right. She opens the door and yells through without departing the room. "He's awake! Nurse! Nurses! Please!" she cries hysterically. "Jaesyk's awake! Help!"

She turns and runs to me, grabbing my face with both hands, pressing the side of her face against my own. I want to bring my hands to her face so badly but can't yet fully move my body. Her face wets mine with tears. I can only hold the inside of her thigh with my hand as I feel her bawl against me.

Immeasurable euphoric relief courses through me.

I made it.

Epilogue

O pening my eyes, I hear the finality of a concussive slam of heavy dense metal at my back. I do not need to peer over my shoulder to investigate. I know well of that sound. I close my eyes and take my time to breathe in deep and exhale in relaxation—to enjoy the atmosphere in reminiscence and reverie.

Several things rush to my mind.

Oh, how I have missed that smile.

Finally here.

I can't wait to get there! To our meeting place, to see that smile again.

I look down as I open my right palm low, at the level just below my hip. A single coin of significance lies there. In exultation, I clench my fist around the coin. I take a step forward and look in the distance as I revel and bring in another deep breath.

There . . . ahead, through the gnarled thicket, shines a faint yellowish ember that pulses slightly as it traverses behind the foreground of leafless dark branches.

A smile is felt as it makes its way across my face. A smile that may rival even the one ahead.

Author's Note

I wanted to tell a story of loyalty and honor. And so, I set off with this character—someone who I knew would do anything to get back to what was most important to them. I wanted this person to be so hell-bent on doing so that they would likely end up being morally gray, possibly to an extreme degree. This intrigued me, the thought and idea that the reader may find themselves questioning if they agree or not with the actions and reactions of Jaesyk while on his quest for return. I knew in order to succeed in this that I had to commit to letting Jaesyk do whatever it took to get back to Nahla, as long as that didn't mean him breaking his own morality and rules.

All in all, I believe I succeeded in what I set out to do—telling this story of loyalty and honor. You may question whether some of Jaesyk's choices were honorable or not, but to him they were. They all were! One of the most rewarding aspects of storytelling and writing for me is getting to the end and seeing for the first time what the characters did and what story THEY told. I generally have an idea of where things may go and what may happen, but that isn't the fun part. The fun comes when characters surprise me with their decisions, and then I get to stand back and look at the manuscript from a bird's-eye view and realize what facets the characters have hidden within that I never even planned on being entwined within it all. I let all these characters flourish and be themselves, and now I can see that this book became more than just Jaesyk's story of loyalty. This book ended up being not a story, but stories—of relationships. All the relationships in *End Realm* ride the tales of either loyalty or betrayal, often to extremes.

There are definitely other facets within *End Realm*, such as journeys of trauma and its long-lasting effects, the paths of depression, and the importance of memory. You may even find a few others, though it's undeniable that these pages hold highest stories of undying loyalty and painful betrayal. Though I also want to note that even the loyalty and friendship of Hades and Karhon is not entirely a relationship without pain and trauma. Loyalty doesn't always mean constant happiness and safety. And betrayal doesn't always mean endless suffering like it unfortunately did for Medusa. My hope is that many of you will—like me—reach the end of these pages and find yourself reflecting, both on the tales in *End Realm* and those that you yourself have carved out, walked, trudged through, and endured in your own lives.

I want to give special thanks to Kaitlyn Katsoupis for some early and much appreciated feedback. Not all of her thoughts resonated with me (such is the way of editorial feedback), though some observations she shared hit with exceptional strength. Kaitlyn pointed out that several of the story's smaller arcs seemed unnecessary, not leading anywhere significant, and . . . it's very possible even after my revisions that she may feel the same. But her feedback made me realize that in these instances she mentioned, I had kept many things to myself. Many things that I realized the reader needed to know in order for those plotlines to feel meaningful. So in these instances, I divulged more of the internal workings within my mind, putting them to the page so you all wouldn't (hopefully) feel them falling flat.

Without her feedback and nudge toward these areas that she felt were falling short, I fear I would have failed in what I most set forth to do with this novel. So, thank you, Kaitlyn! For your brutal honesty and insight.

Thank you to all my beta readers, who undoubtedly made it through some very early and rough pages. You all were amazing, and all the feedback, both positive and constructive, was a tremendous help and much appreciated. Michael Welch, Nicole, Jeffrey Nichols, Sierra Zellner, thank you! An additional shout goes again to Sierra Zellner for writing some of my web and general copy text. You're awesome.

I can't even put into words how thankful I am for my amazing editor, Chelsea K. Thank you for catching all my mishaps and blunders. I am eternally grateful for your expertise, your great and concise edit notations, and our mutual love for the almighty—and supreme—em dash! I look forward to working together again, and . . . I'm sorry in advance!

Thanks to Steve Stred, the absolute voracious reader and writer, for making the time in your crazy schedule to read *End Realm* and give such a badass blurb after. Thanks, dude. I'll never forget! And to Robin Knabel at Inky Bones Press for doing the same. I know both your schedules are crushing, and I appreciate beyond words that you made sure there was room for *End Realm*.

Thanks to Adam L.G. Nevill, for sharing his incredible stories and writing with the world. I find that so many authors today shy from poetic literary description and exposition. I believe it's in fear of boring their readers, fear of being redundant, and also wanting to meet their editors' suggestions on long winded and purple prose. I however have an affinity for such writing, one that I find nears infatuation. Your writing reinforces and validates for me that crafting such prose is not only okay, but something I should encourage within my own journey of bettering my craft. Thank you for inspiring me, for staying humble as fuck even in your exponential success, for the bits of advice on publishing, and again for sharing all the dark, dreary, and deep tales with us.

To my loving parents, Theone and Michael Welch, who never once stifled my creativity or ambitions.

To my lovely wife, Nicole, the graphic designer and artist. For your love and support in everything I venture forth into. To our two amazing sons, Carson and Zayne, for all the fun, laughs, and games. I thank all three of you for showing me patience while I write for hours at a time and for making life so damn incredibly worth living. Nicole, Carson, Zayne, I love you!

I hope you all have found the hidden light within the darkness of these pages. And thank you for joining me in the depths of this particular afterlife.

—Tyler J. Welch